CVC

CVC

Carter V. Cooper

SHORT FICTION ANTHOLOGY SERIES

BOOK THREE

SELECTED BY, AND WITH A PREFACE BY

Gloria Vanderbilt

Library and Archives Canada Cataloguing in Publication

CVC : Carter V. Cooper short fiction anthology series : book three /
edited by Gloria Vanderbilt.

(CVC : Carter V. Cooper short fiction anthology series ; bk. 3)
ISBN 978-1-55096-357-1

1. Short stories, Canadian (English). 2. Canadian fiction (English)--21st
century. I. Vanderbilt, Gloria, 1924- II. Series: Carter V. Cooper short fiction
anthology series ; bk. 3

PS8329.1.C833 2013   C813'.010806   C2013-903467-6

Copyright © with the Authors, and Exile Editions, 2013
Design and Composition by Hourglass Angels mc
Typeset in Garamond, Mona Lisa and Trajan fonts
Printed by Imprimerie Gauvin

Published by Exile Editions Ltd ~ www.ExileEditions.com
144483 Southgate Road 14 – GD, Holstein, Ontario, N0G 2A0
Printed and Bound in Canada in 2013

The publisher would like to acknowledge the financial support of the Canada
Council for the Arts, the Government of Canada through the Canada Book
Fund (CBF), the Ontario Arts Council, and the Ontario Media Development
Corporation, for our publishing activities.

Any inquiries regarding publication rights, translation rights, or film rights
should be directed to: info@exileeditions.com

Canadian Sales: The Canadian Manda Group, 165 Dufferin Street,
Toronto ON M6K 3H6   www.mandagroup.com   416 516 0911

North American and international Distribution, and U.S. Sales:
Independent Publishers Group, 814 North Franklin Street,
Chicago IL 60610   www.ipgbook.com   toll free: 1 800 888 4741

In memory of

Carter V. Cooper

The Winners for Year Three

Best Story by an Emerging Writer
≈ $10,000 ≈

Sang Kim

Best Story by a Writer at Any Point of Career
≈ Sharing the $5,000 ≈

Priscila Uppal and Austin Clarke

CVC

Book Three

PREFACE

This annual short fiction competition is open to all Canadian writers, with two prizes awarded: $10,000 for the best story by an emerging writer, and $5,000 for the best story by a writer at any point of her/his career. Hundreds of stories were received in 2012–13, and from the 12 that eventually were shortlisted, I selected the winners, being those that most appealed to me, as a writer, as a reader, and as a lover of the written word on paper. And, like the first two years, I simply could not choose only two. About the winners, I have this to say: Sang Kim's "When John Lennon Died" takes the Emerging prize with a story about loss. Loss as defined by the Welsh word *hiraeth*: "a homesickness for a home to which you cannot return, a home which maybe never was; the nostalgia, the yearning, the grief for the lost places of your past. It is told with courage and restraint, making it all the more powerful. A brilliant debut. "Cover Before Striking" by Priscila Uppal shares the Writer at Any Career Point prize: my heart raced with anger and fear as I read. At moments I was afraid to continue, but so beautifully crafted – original, disturbing, poetic – it pulled me on. And Austin Clarke's "They Never Told Me" is a mesmerizing, haunting story that springs with life from the page to reach the deepest places in the mind and heart. A story we will not forget.

I am proud and thrilled that all these wonderful writers are presented in the *CVC Short Fiction Anthology–Book Three,* a special edition published in memory of my son, Carter V. Cooper.

And I want to give a big *Thank You* to the readers who adjudicated this competition: Matt Shaw, Susan Walker, and Barry Callaghan... all who have played their own special roles in the development and support of emerging writers.

Gloria Vanderbilt

Gloria Vanderbilt
May, 2013

WHEN JOHN LENNON DIED

In the winter of 1980, when I was twelve and a police order kept my father away, Tom Chang, a deacon at my mother's church, visited our home every weekend. This was in Koreatown, near Bloor and Christie, and my father had put all of our savings into a convenience store because he believed that our luck was going to change and that fortune would finally come our way. My mother changed the locks after the last incident with my father and my five-year-old brother was sent to stay with my grandmother until things settled down.

Tom Chang was married with three children. One of them was a girl my own age, Sabrina, who was always so upbeat at our Sunday school that I had assumed she knew nothing about her father's weekend visits. I may have been wrong about this; maybe Sabrina did know, but as a good Christian she had faith that it was all a part of God's plan.

This was around the time John Lennon died and although I could not confirm it to be true, both my mother and Tom talked about him as though he was their friend. One night, they sat around the kitchen table listening to his music on the radio. My mother swirled whiskey in her glass while Tom kept time to the music by tapping his feet on the linoleum. And when he sang along to some of the tunes, his high-pitched voice was so different from my father's that I thought he sounded like a girl and not a real man.

My mother spoke in Korean to both of us, but Tom spoke to me only in English. He had studied in Canada and I remember my mother being very pleased when she told me this.

"He wrote this after he left the Beatles," Tom said during one song. The singer's voice had a raw and hurting feeling to it like he was crying out to somebody who was leaving him or had left him already. I asked Tom what the song was about.

"Oh, about loss," he said. My mother rose from her chair and stood at the kitchen window. Her arms were wrapped around her chest and she was looking at the drifting snow.

"It's late," my mother said. "Go to bed."

"But it's Saturday," I said. Tom laughed and put his hand behind my head and pulled me towards him like he was going to tell me a secret but, instead, he put a dollar bill in my hand.

"Go out and buy yourself a comic book," he said, and winked at me. We sold Archie comics at our convenience store, but I never liked reading them because there were no heroes in them.

It was also around this time, that a brown Buick Riviera began to appear on our side street. I knew who owned all the cars on Euclid Avenue, at least the ones south of Bloor Street, and nobody owned a Buick Riviera. It would be there before I went to bed and be gone before I left for school the next morning. After dinner, I would watch from my bedroom window as the car pulled up slowly, like it was driving over broken glass, and park in front of Jake DiNardi's house just beyond the street lamp. In the weeks following Lennon's death, the car came around more than usual. Through my binoculars, I could see the outline of a man leaning forward in the driver's seat, looking up at my mother's room. I could tell it was a man by his body size; he was as big as my father and seemed to take up the whole front of the car.

When I went outside to buy the comic book with the money Tom had given me, the car was there as usual. The headlights were turned off but I could tell that the engine was still running from the white smoke coming out of the exhaust. I thought that the man inside must have been cold and had kept the engine on to stay warm. I crossed to the other side of the street. When the car was directly to my left, I took a quick look but could only see the back of the man's head.

I returned later with a copy of *G.I. Joe* tucked inside my coat and the car was still there, but the engine was shut off. A thin layer of snow covered the car, so I could not tell if someone was inside. A television set flickered in Jake's living room and I knew that he and his brothers were sitting around eating pizzas and watching *Hockey Night in Canada* like they did every Saturday night. I approached the car slowly and could hear the snow crunching under my boots. I wiped some snow off the passenger-side window and leaned in to look. On the seat there was what looked like a baseball bat and a pair of binoculars like my own, except they were much bigger. Suddenly, I felt someone standing behind me and was surprised to hear a sound like a drowning person coming out my mouth. I turned around to face him and recognized him as the owner of the car even though I had never seen his face before. He was a big white man wearing a bomber jacket and his leather gloves looked almost too small on his hands. The light in my mother's bedroom was on and I wanted to call out to her, but my mouth would not open.

"It's okay, kid," the man said. His breath was bluish in the air. "I'm not gonna hurt you. I just want to talk." He bent down to look into my eyes and I could see that his face was full of tiny craters. A scar the size of a caterpillar ran under his chin.

"You like my car?" he said. I shrugged my shoulders because I wasn't sure if I liked his car or not. "It's cold out here. Why don't we go in—" And before he could finish what he was saying, I made a run for the house. My *G.I. Joe* comic had slipped out of my jacket, but I just left it and kept running. When I reached my front door, I exhaled for the first time and looked back. The man was gone and his car was driving away, down our street. I saw the tail lights brightening at a stop sign before accelerating again.

Upstairs, the radio was still on in the kitchen but my mother and Tom were not there. I went down the narrow cold hallway toward my room and slowed down in front of my mother's bedroom. There was no light under her door and I could hear Tom saying something in a low voice and my mother giggling in a way I wasn't used to hearing from her. I went into my bedroom and lay on my bed. I wondered if the man and his Buick Riviera had anything to do with Tom being at our house all the time, and if the police were ever going to allow my father to return if he promised to never hurt my mother again.

In the morning, I could hear Tom walking past my room and down the staircase. When I looked out the window, he was not on the sidewalk and I heard a car squealing down the icy street but was not sure whose car it was. In the kitchen, my mother was frying eggs and humming to herself. She seemed happier than usual. I didn't tell her about meeting the man outside because I didn't want to ruin her mood. She put a plate of eggs in front of me and went downstairs to open the store. I went out into the street looking for my comic book and found it on the sidewalk buried in the snow. When I came back inside, the telephone was ringing. I picked up the receiver. It was a woman's voice speaking in Korean and she sounded upset about something.

"Where is she?" she said. I asked her if she was looking for my mother and she repeated herself, "Where is she?" I told her that my mother was downstairs watching the store. She hung up without saying goodbye. The woman sounded like an older version of Sabrina. And although I had never spoken to Sabrina's mother before, I thought that their voices would be similar because they were mother and daughter.

After an hour or so, I went downstairs to get a can of pop. The store was empty and my mother was sitting on a stool behind the counter. I could tell she had been crying and she turned away when she saw me.

"I have to go to the hospital," she said after a long time. "You stay here." Her eyes were red and her voice crackly just like it got when my father used to hit her. I had watched the store by myself before, but it was only for short periods of time like when my mother needed to take a washroom break. I sensed my mother would be gone much longer but I didn't bother mentioning that. She put on her coat and hurried out the door.

The neighbours were surprised to see me there by myself and helped me out whenever I didn't know the price of something, like canned tomatoes or shampoo. But I remembered the prices for most things like milk and bread and lottery tickets. Later, Jake dropped by because he had heard that I was alone and wanted to help. I knew he was just saying that and that he really wanted something for free, but I didn't mind because we could talk about things like the hockey game and superheroes and not about the kind of things that were going on in my house. When it was time for him to go home, Jake took a chocolate bar and a bag of chips with him. The store was slower at night because the snow was beginning to really come down.

I was refilling the milk fridge when the telephone rang. When I said "Hello," there was no answer on the other end, just loud music in the background. I was ready to hang up when someone finally spoke. It was my father and I was happy to hear his voice, although I could not tell whether he was happy to hear mine. He asked how I was and I told him I was fine and that I was watching the store by myself because my mother was at the hospital visiting a friend. He told me that he was proud of me and then asked about my younger brother, so I told him he was with our grandmother.

"When are you coming home?" I said.

"Soon," he said. I wanted to ask him if he knew anything about the man and the Buick Riviera but decided not to because I felt like his mind was somewhere else.

"I have to go," he said. "Everything is going to be okay." I didn't know what he meant by that or if I believed that everything was going to be okay or not. All I knew was that things were not like they used to be and might never be again and that I missed my brother, even though he bothered me sometimes.

When I got off the telephone with my father, I tore open a bag of chips and looked outside. It was like someone had dropped a white blanket over the storefront. I could not see any cars or people passing by, so I imagined everybody in their homes with people they loved and who loved them back. I wasn't sure if my mother was going to come back any time soon, so I walked myself through closing up the store. The most important part was to take the money out of the cash register and put it in the brown bag behind the ice freezer.

It was very late when my mother came home. I was at the kitchen table doing my homework. Her eyes were red and she looked tired. She went to the sink to pour herself a drink and asked me about my day. I told her everything went fine but not the part about Jake dropping by and taking food with him, even though I never said he could. I also wanted to tell her that my father had called, but I felt like she already knew.

"Get some sleep," she said. "You have school tomor-row." I asked her if Tom was going to come by. She turned away from me and took a big sip of her whiskey.

"No," she said. "He's not." She then asked me if I liked Tom.

"Yes." I lied because I knew it would make her feel better if I said that. She told me that he liked me too, liked me very much, but that he was probably never going to come to our house again. She was quiet for a long time and then she let out an exhaling sound, like the sound of a cat I had once heard when it was run over by a car. I could tell there was a lot on her mind so I got up to go to bed. I said good night to her from my bedroom door, but I don't think she heard me. She was sitting there at the table staring at the wall.

I awoke to banging on the front door. I got out of bed and looked out my window. It was very dark even though there was a lot of snow outside. I could not see anyone because the front door was on the same side as my window. When he raised his voice, I could tell it was my father and that he had been drinking, but I couldn't make out anything he was saying. Some lights came on in the houses across the street. I imagined my mother with her ear pressed against her bedroom door and holding the doorknob like a grenade ready to explode. My father sounded angry and he kept saying things to my mother as though she was standing in front of him but far away. I returned to my bed after the police came and took my father away. I lay there for a while thinking about my mother and whether or not I should go into her room. I knew that some bad things were happening to her now and that more bad things would happen to her again, but I did not feel sorry for her. As I began falling asleep, I thought about all the snow and my brother who was staying with my grandmother and how things didn't seem quite right in the world. John Lennon had died and I knew that it would be a long time before his death didn't mean anything to me anymore.

George McWhirter

TENNIS

They tell me, report nothing, Gene. That how they say
Jean. Report nothing or they think you the one
involved, and you become the suspect. You try help this
guy, broken up in some accident, and they sue you for
fix him up. Like, even if you arc an MD Surgeon – you
keep out, or else you spend your holiday in the police
station, making the statement. Somebody sue the boots
off your feet, and you go no place.

Something about a bad dose of Napoleonic Law
Mexicans got. We have the good recipe for it in
Quebec, but here, the Napoleonic Law sort of got the
shits. Like from the fruit, too much heat.

That what I think about the run-over guy. Don't
look up close. And I think, why the car not make it
over his head? An auto leave a big impression on a
guy's head. Like cat you see on the highway – flat. Like
pizza with the hair topping. But this head is still one
piece and the res' – neck, ches', knee, an' his ankle –
run over.

Damn taxi driver stop for nothing, I think. They
jus' run him over, one after the other. Too busy to make
the stop in case they miss the next fare. This too much,

I tell Rose-Marie. I pull him up, I put him against the door of that *Club de Tenís*.

From Adam, I don't know this one guy. But me, I feel sad for him, and the love charm he have on his gold bracelet. I know it.

Since we been in Acapulco, we are buying pretty heavy. We work hard for the good deal in silver or gold off the beach vendor. Make the bid, wait one day or two, see it drop. Anyway, I watch the jewellery and I ask people what price and where they buying. I remember the good jewellery, and I know it on the guy. For sure, because you know, I see his partner put that there gold bracelet on the wrist of that run-over guy.

This late night – 11 p.m. The shore patrol from the Hornos base, they come, and they are stepping into the gateway and into the doorway. They go look-see, like the garbage men in Montréal. Then, the run-over guy, he say, "Vamoose," like they do in the movie. Rose-Marie and I figure they must be two sailor, who sneak in the *Club de Tenís* for some back and forth with the ball – and the bracelet, it for some bet what the one guy win.

"Two handsome guy," say Rose-Marie, "and that bracelet with the love charm heart look pretty good to this old bird."

Morning and afternoon, lotsa women go in there, to the *Club de Tenís*. Handsome, well-preserve women like Rose-Marie. When the limo leave them. they show a lot of the leg in white short. Lot of brown Mexican leg. It make you want to hit that furry ball, whip that feather birdie all day. This what one of the two sailor is twirl – white cork head of that feather birdie wit' his finger. And while one is kissing his bracelet with the love charm heart – this other sailor is suck the cork on his birdie.

I touch this here lucky charm that he kiss, but Rose-Marie is giving me the instruction, "Jean Rubinsky, the police," and "Jean Rubinsky, the ambulance"; and I say, "I take no gold heart off this sailor." I touch his lucky charm like I say sorry for you, sailor; I sure would like to know you better. An' I wan' tell him some thing – like I know you are one cute guy, an' my Rose-Marie not mind to have you in her bed. But, I sure as hell glad some taxi make the pizza out of you first.

Now, Rose-Marie, she want me to telephone. "Jean, you make the report to this Mr. Tiger. Jean, you can tell it to him in French, tell him in the English. Jean, in Mexican, like it say in the paper." Now, Rose-Marie read it and I read it in the *Montréal Magazine*, about this Hot-Dog-Eater Chief of Police. Ex-Mountie, Manitoba, then Montréal, then Acapulco. He say Montréal get too crazy with the violence, and why just be the constable or sergeant in Montréal when he qualify for Chief and get more pay for give the criminals target practice in Acapulco.

And on top, he have family here in Acapulco, and he have this licence from the UNAM. Some guy tell me it the Mexico university, not United Nations, and I think – the Hot Dog Eater is educated man. He listen. He know I got no beef with this road accident. I take no bracelet. I take a look is all – jus' make sure the guy is the one I see kissing the other guy before Hornos shore patrol catch them. Big Mexican *abrazo* – each guy suck the other up, like two Pepsi on one hot-damn day.

"But this run-over guy still got his wallet," I tell Rose-Marie. "This mean he is jus' run-over. Not no victim in no robbery."

"Ah-oui," Rose-Marie, she yell at me – *"ne touches pas ça!"*

Okay, I got my fingerprint on the dead sailor wallet. I rub them off, but that when I remember what like I see from the corridor back of our room. I waiting for Rose-Marie to finish fix the hair. That corridor got windows that look inland and I got my big glasses that can see all the way to Japan.

It morning and the *Club de Tenís* get lotsa light from the east and I see the run-over sailor and this other sailor wrestle in their tennis short. On the tennis court – on the roof, they do like that lambada. One of them get the other from behind and he hold him. Hand in his pant, for squeeze him, like kids do when they play like they are mad at each other. Except Rose-Marie, she tell me, now that she have a good look, now that she have the hair combed out of her eye, "*Ils sont fou d'amour,*" crazy in love.

Two ladies come out, start play, make pretty shot. They bend for pick up the ball and look at them two sailor, to watch see a smile at their nice move with that bat and the ball. Now, those guy are off each other back. And, the two sailor boy smile at the women like the women are the ice cream and their tongue keep one special lick for them.

Then, I remember I see the run-over guy, one night, at the *Club de Tenís*. He shove out the door. He rock up and down on the *Club de Tenís* sidewalk, which is all wreck with the truck and with the taxi. The sailor boy slip, and he turn, yell good and loud at this ol' man in this Mexican shirt. You know them silk shirt, like jacket with pocket. That old guy, he hold that other shipmate – his sailor friend, he hold him by the arm. He say, "*Puto, no tokay.*" Then, he yell, "*No tokay o te mato.*"

"*Tokay*, temato," that what he say. He as mad as Rose-Marie when I touch the wallet to find this run-over guy name.

I confess. I got this one habit. I sneak big sun-downer before Rose-Marie finish the siesta. I go to the lobby, talk to the porter, then I go down the street see what new at the *Club de Tenís*. That when I see the old guy.

One of the Anglos at La Copa and me, we watch that melee between this angry old guy and those two sailor. Anglo tell me, "You find those fags, fucked to death at your feet, don't interfere! That there is a love triangle. Old gentleman there is keeping that young one he's got by the arm and he is pissed at his new play-mate. Mexicans fix problems like that with guns. Don't interfere."

"Me," I say. "One guy be eating the balls of the other guy on a plate, and all I say is *bon appétit!*"

But Rose-Marie say I nosier than her mother. "Fact, her mother love me more than Rose-Marie for I got all this stuff to tell.

The old guy I see one, maybe two time more. He have the condo down this street by the beach. I see him drive in, Friday, 8 p.m., then, Monday, 7 – 'e drive out same. Same thing nex' Friday an' Monday.

You bet I watch. Giving the eyeball a refill with jus' sunshine get boring, if you got one month to kill. You bet I get to watch this street like it my neigh-bourhood.

This old guy, he got his condo so he be near the big naval base. Anyway, that time in the street, when they play the love triangle. It a real dingdong match. The old guy take the black ball for the squash. He squeeze his thumb in it, and he flick it in the face of the run-over guy. He take the birdie thing and he squish it on the run-over guy head.

But the run-over guy, he too flat and bad beat-up for that birdie or some ping-pong bat to be the murder weapon.

Anyway, we go get taxi and tell this Mr. Tiger guy. We tell him what I tell you, Clement. Them Mexican at the desk lick up our French, like it ice cream, but they talk English back. The Acapulco Mountie, he talk French good, and he talk it until we go back and we see this *cadaver* with all the Mexican cop in Acapuko stare at it Then, he not talk, he say nothing in Mexican or English.

"*Merci,*" he say for the statement, "*merci,*" for the old guy description. For the condo informations, the informations about the birdie and squash ball that the ol' guy squeeze. "*Merci. J'aime le Québec, c'est pour les raisons de famille que je suis de retour au Mexique.*"

He say all this in French, like he talk to himself. He has this wife, a Mexican woman, and her family not like the police – detective of the police, no better. She think Mexican police are the criminals, he say. He say he tell her we go to Canada where the police have respect, and he study, and he work so he can make RCMP, but the wife, she stay in Mexico with the son. See what happen to him, Mr. Tiger, in *le Canada*, first.

Next thing, he tell me she say she divorce him. So, he come down for get back the respect of his son. And he still pay so his wife can eat *les petit-fours*, et *les entrecôtes*. "Now," he say, "I will see you and Rose-Marie to your hotel, Jean, and you will have the protection of my department."

"Why we need the protection?" Rose-Marie ask. And when she see the big tear in Mr. Tiger eye, she think it because the hot dog eater not be able to protect us. We are in some hot shit.

"We stop go out late. If we lose the nightlife, we are having the pleasure of the morning, Firs' light – up. But morning is good time to make the hit. No people. Only fishermens in the boat that pull in the net. And any assassin follow our footprint, easy – in the sand." I tell Rose-Marie so every time we walk over where the little guy from the hotel rake the san'. "But this is dumb, Jean," Rose-Marie say. "Other people out for the walk mix up their mark with our mark in the sand."

Rose-Marie pretend she is the brave one, but for two, three day we are real scared. Everything look bigger than I ever see it. We see this small hairy fish that got big head and whisker like Rose-Marie maman. Fat head you can't tell from the body, with the big cut 'cross it, like some speedboat hit it good with the propeller. I see the sun make the hair stick out on Rose-Marie face. Québec women sure have the bristle. They take the electrolysis for kill the hair on their faces, an' they don't show moustache. If we get back, I make that the present for Rose-Marie. But we see no cop, no criminal no place, but how we tell undercover cop from criminal?

When fish boats come in, chef from the bistros go pick in the boat for the good fish. They make the bargain. This morning we see the demonstration at this boat that lie way up on the sand. We say, for sure – they buy the fish. Only the other guys, the shore patrol guys, they come. They are looking for the sailor that get drunk and not make it back to base. They look under the boat for them, like the people from the bistro look for the fish, inside.

Or shore patrol buy fish this morning, 'cause they bored for not find guys go AWOL. For now they are poke in the boat with *les chefs* bistro. And me, I got the blister on my bare feet from the tough brown sand here and I am real glad to make the stop. I don't know what the matter with that sand. Maybe the sea make her too quick and not grind her up right.

"*Jean, dépêche-toi,*" Rose-Marie say when she see the feet that stick out of that boat. Feet that are cover in one big cake of this crazy ginger sand.

Rose-Marie, she have the front row. "Jean, this the other, the not run-over guy," she shout at me. "Jean, Jean," she shout.

One big argument go on with the shore patrol and the guy who own that boat. The shore patrol point at what in the dead guy mouth, what stick out with the wet feather. Sure this thing have feather, but for sure is no seagull. The shore patrol, they pull it out and the top has turned brown with the blood, like the end of the hot dog dip in ketchup.

Rose-Marie, she choke, but she say, "See." And all those guys see loud and clear.

But ACAPULCO TIMES say it is this:

The son of Police Chief Tigre and the son of the Mayor of Igualada have been found dead two days apart. Both were doing their military service at Horno's base and both were able-bodied seamen. Although recent elections in Guerrero have recorded fewer murders, these deaths are considered political and designed as warnings for the Mayor and Chief of Police, who are known to be independents and who stop at nothing to see justice done. The Mayor was not available for comment, and when interviewed, Alonso Tigre, said that all kinds of love speak their name in Mexico nowadays, but the one that must bite its lip is the love of freedom and fair play. "My loss is your loss, that is how democracy works. A crime committed by one is like a mistake made by all."

We got all kinds of same stuff in Québec. We keep what we seen from the Mexico reporters. I tell you, Clement, this what is happen. It no love triangle, like the Anglo say. This what I learn in geomentry, long time ago. This a love quadrangle – for those two son and two poppas, they square off. You get the big picture, Clement – guys who got sons gotta be the policeman nowaday.

After it all over, we still got two week and *Noel*. We have the Christmas turkey in the Copacabango. But out there on the big deck with all that water rush at the hotel, turkey that the chef carve not look right size. It shrink or something. We don't know. Rose-Marie and me, we don't like eat turkey outdoor. The fresh pineapple, cut up, is better. It look jus' right.

David Somers

PUNCHY
SELLS OUT

The door opened. It was Limpy Spence.

"Hi, Ed."

"Limpy."

"How's it goin'?" Pete said.

"Hi, Pete. Didya hear?" Limpy asked.

"No. What?" I asked.

Limpy came over from the front of the shop, his boots tripping on the checkered floor tiles. He sat down squirming and on edge. It was just like always, only more so.

He leaned forward, bursting: "You'll never guess."

"Tell me," I said. Limpy stopped for a second and caught his breath. I looked in the mirror. "A little bit more around the ears, Pete."

"I'm workin' on it, Ed," Pete mumbled.

"You'll never believe this, Ed. You, too, Pete."

"So tell us, Limpy" we said.

It was always the same with Limpy: enough to drive lesser men to violence. He took a deep breath and straightened up. "Punchy's selling out."

It was as simple as that, but Limpy had to say it again. "Punchy's selling out."

Pete stopped his work, dangerously leaving me in mid-haircut.

"Punchy's selling out?" I asked.

"Punchy is selling out," Limpy said again with a slight nod and a half-witted smile. He sat back in the chair and ran his skeleton hands back through his tobacco-washed pompadour.

"Chrissakes, eh?"

"Who'd ever a-thought, eh?" Pete said. He had stopped work completely and was staring out the front window.

"We'll just hafta see about all this then," I said. "Let's go, Pete."

Pete started up his work again. He was making a fine job of it despite the news. Pete had reached a critical point. He applied a straight razor to the back of my neck and around my sideburns, pulling away hot shaving foam and stubble with long, steady strokes. Limpy watched Pete work. Through the mirror, I watched Pete work. From a jar of alcohol, he pulled a long wooden skewer, the end bound tightly with a wad of cotton. He struck a match and set fire to the cotton. Pete sent the slender torch across my earlobes, nostrils, and cheeks with a series of deft figure-eight moves, instantly ridding me of thousands of fine hairs.

Limpy's mouth hung open in wonder. A course of shampooing, rinsing, conditioning, and repeat rinsing followed. Pete took a fresh towel off the radiator, wrapped it loosely around my head and face and worked it around my hair to dry it completely. He scrubbed out my ears and then finished up with a punishing massage of my scalp, temples, neck, and shoulders. He poured a couple of shots of aftershave into his cupped palms and slapped them hard across my face. Pure craftsmanship. Pete, whose real name was Anton, had served his decade-long apprenticeship under the oppressive guidance of the master Turkish barber, Mustafa of Fethiye. The celebrated Mustafa had been a barber above all other barbers, and newspapers reported that hundreds of thousands of barbers turned out to follow his funeral cortege, with many running up to the casket to touch it with their white towels, and some placing scissors and combs alongside the body, and others throwing hair cuttings under the wheels of the open hearse, and hundreds fainting and thousands more wailing in anguish, and barbers round the world wept for weeks, and in that time you couldn't get a haircut for love nor money. A great race for barbering, the Turks.

Anyways, Pete was good, maybe one of the best. He always made a fine job of it, but he wouldn't stand a chance around here if Punchy sold out. Even Limpy Spence knew that.

I stood up out of the great leather chair. Pete brushed off my clothes and helped me on with my jacket.

I looked in the mirror. Pete had delivered a classic Banchoff-Klein cut. I turned my head slightly from side to side. Perfect.

"You've made a fine job of it, Pete," I said.

"It's a fine job," Limpy said.

I paid Pete. I gave him a generous tip, too. We shook hands.

"Let's go find out what this is all about, Limpy," I said.

"Tell me what you hear," Pete said. He was worried. Limpy and I could hear it in his voice.

Limpy and I left the shop and stepped out into the street. A bloody hot day it was, and dusty, too. Wind blew the dust around, and a yellow film of sulphur and smoke obscured the sun. Bad luck days. All the signs were there. We looked up and down the street: a long dirt road lined with a haphazard collection of shoddy buildings on each side. That was the street, and that was the town. Two long lines of bunk houses and ale houses, cat houses and out houses, hen houses and store houses, gaming houses, alms houses, cook houses, play houses, and an Orange Lodge. Men crowded the street, moving from one place to the next. At one end of the road was the rail station. At the other was the company's industrial site, a sprawling complex of yard office, smokestacks, cranes, furnaces, workshops, refuse heaps, cesspools, and heavy machinery. Halfway between the company site and the rail station was Punchy's place.

Limpy was nervous. He kept staring after me, maybe looking for some reassurance, maybe that I was going to tell him that it was going to be all right, maybe that the news wouldn't mean nothing at all, maybe that I had a plan and we'd be okay.

"What's going to happen d'ya think, Ed?"

I said nothing. The effects of the haircut were beginning to wear off already in the heat and dust. Little drops of sweat fell off the end of my nose and disappeared in the dust at my boots. My shirt clung to my back and arms. I felt a bit dizzy and wanted to sit down on the edge of the boardwalk. I tried to focus. Feet flat, eyes front, shoulders back, mind clear, I told myself.

"Let's go."

We walked out into the street. I marched forward as steadily as I could under the circumstances. Limpy skipped and shuffled beside me, stirring up dust as we went. Poor wreck, I thought. Limpy was a knock-kneed, bow-legged, pigeon-toed shambles of a man with a face like a fireman's axe, but he had the purest heart of any man I had ever known, and that made him alright in my books. He was my friend.

We continued up the street, walking without benefit of shade or shelter from the dust and wind. We stopped.

"Punchy's," I said. We stood for a moment in front of Punchy's place. With its boomtown façade and grand front entrance, it had staked a claim of importance in town, and it was all that and more for us. Everything a man in these parts could need or want, he could get it at Punchy's. Everyone came to Punchy's, and Punchy's was home to everyone.

We walked in.

It was just like it always was, only this time it was different. The place was packed, but it was strangely quiet. No music, no loud arguments, no laughter. I picked out Punchy from the crowd. He looked up at us and nodded. I nodded back. Limpy and I made our way through the crowd and sat at a table near the bar. Punchy came over and waited on us himself.

"Boys."

"Punchy," I said.

"The special?"

"The special," I said.

"Right. Two specials," Punchy said. He knew that we knew, but none of us said anything. He went to the kitchen to pass our order on to the cook.

Limpy stared at the tabletop, his long fingers tracing the dark lines in the wood grain. I looked around. Lots of guys I knew. Irving Whale. Chester Various. Jesus Murphy. Red Starr. Goldberg and McCann. Not much talking going on. Not much of anything. Just a lot of hung faces pouring back the long draught. Over in the corner two Latvian woodcutters I knew, Ozol and Lindenberg, sat drinking Black Balsam and eating sausage, every now and then sharing something in that peculiar dead language of theirs. Wild wavy white hair flowed back from the crown of each man's head. Like two lost emperors they sat, daring anyone to trespass on their territory or conversation. But good men with a saw or an axe they were. A great race for woodcutting, the Latvian.

After a couple of minutes, Punchy came back with two specials. Limpy and I dug into our porterhouse steaks and pan-fried potatoes and baked beans and washed down each mouthful with steaming black coffee. We helped ourselves to the side-plates heaped with beef sausages and pork cutlets and roast chicken and rashers of bacon. We didn't feel much like eating, but we knew we had to for Punchy's sake. We had apple pie and ice cream, too – for Punchy. Limpy had a few cookies and a milkshake. I had a beer. Limpy considered ordering an Eccles cake and a glass of blueberry juice.

We didn't want to eat, but what's a guy supposed to do when Punchy's selling out? Anyone would do the same as us.

Limpy had a second helping of ice cream. For Punchy.

"We know," I said when Punchy came back over with the cigar I had asked for.

"I know you know, boys," Punchy said.

We fell quiet. Punchy stood by our table and looked out past the customers to the big plate-glass window at the front where "PUNCHY'S" was spelled out. I chewed on a few pretzels and drew on the cigar. Limpy watched the last bits of his ice cream melt away in the dish.

"The company's closing the line, boys. They've used up everything around here that they can, and they're packin' it in. They sent out the notices an hour ago. That means this whole town's finished. A couple of company agents came by and offered me ten cents on the dollar for all my inventory that I can't sell by the end of tomorrow. Same thing with the building – they bought the salvage rights. They'll knock it down and ship the lumber off to the next place. They're makin' the one-time-only offer to everyone on the street, and none of us can afford to turn them down. With no company, there's no workers. No workers mean there's no customers. It's as simple as that, boys. We're sellin' out."

Punchy looked like he was going to apologize or something.

"I gotta cut my losses, boys. Besides, youse'll be packin' up and leavin' before the week's out anyways what with the company closin' the line. There's nothin' left for any one of us here."

"So that's it," I said.

"That's it," Punchy said.

Guys like Punchy were one in a half a million. It didn't matter what company owned how much of any town we were in, it only mattered that a guy like Punchy would come along and open up a place where everyone else could come to and feel human. We live our lives in places like this, forgetting the back-break and the grind that waited for us down at the end of the road behind the company walls.

I remember the first time I set eyes on the heaping slab of meat I would learn was Punchy. Limpy and I had just arrived in town, brought in by rumours of work. We were hungry, we were cold, and we knew no one. But once we walked through those doors and sat down to a steak and a whiskey and warmed ourselves over by the fireplace, I knew that we had found as much as a home as we'd ever have. Punchy, with a greying crewcut more severe than any I'd ever seen, had set us up in lodgings and steered us towards someone in the company who'd hire us on. "It's self-interest," Punchy'd told me at the time. "Guys like you'll hang around this place and spend good money here."

"So you're really selling, eh?" I said. "Can't believe it."

"Closin' the line, too," Punchy said. "Hafta tell ya, it was just a matter of time. Happens everywhere. When they've taken all they can from one place, they move on to the next before their profits dip. Can't expect anything else, really. We'd do the same if we were in their shoes."

"We're all finished," Limpy said.

Limpy and I sat in silence for a while longer, and Punchy went back to his work. I got up, put money on the table for our meals and told Limpy I'd meet him in a while down at our bunkhouse. I went outside.

Limpy was partly right. He was finished. Once guys like him get pushed out the door, it's next to impossible to find work again. Myself, I still had my health. Plus I had years of experience doing just about everything. At one time or another I'd been a privateer, a Volunteer, a grenadier, a fusilier. I'd been a soldier, a scholar, a barroom brawler, a hand on a trawler, a midnight caller. I'd been a man about town, a circus clown, a robber, a jobber, known through the land, known as yer man, straight on the narrow, true to the marrow. I'd been a physician, a surgeon, a doctor, a quack, doling out pills and a pat on the back. I could take care of myself. Limpy, on the other hand, was finished.

I walked up the street in the direction of the company yard. Along the way I passed a brass band playing for spare change. The musicians all had long greasy hair and tatty uniforms, and they produced such a painful bawling sound that I wondered if they hadn't stolen the instruments that very morning. I stopped and looked into the open cardboard case they had in front of them on the ground: a few pencil stubs, an old comb, three pennies and a gob of spit.

"Play the changes, you morons," I said, but they kept right on with their noise. "Bloody Schoenberg," I grumbled as I walked away.

Already signs were being posted on doors and in windows advertising closing-out sales. Owners of other businesses were loading their goods and furniture onto truck and wagons, tarping everything over and tying everything down. There wasn't any panic, just a sense of resignation.

I walked in through the main gates of the company yard. The last shift was still going full speed. Smoke stacks spewed heavy clouds of black and yellow, and cranes swung back and forth. Cascades of sparks shot from the yawning black doorways of the works buildings. Slag and tailings continued to pile up. The air was thick with the smell of coal and sulphur, and it scraped at the eyes and poisoned the throat. A roaring din hammered at the eardrums, clashing and clanging around the inside of every man's head. The landscape had been scoured bare for miles around. We had made our mark.

Shaved-headed company security guards were littered throughout the site, keeping watch for last minute acts of sabotage and theft. They were more heavily armed than usual and walked in groups of not less than three.

From the inside of one building came the alternating thunder and scream of a Van Rooyen Special, its valves deliberately jammed open by its operator. I knew that engine well, having run a couple away back in the old Nag Copaleen Works, and there was no mistaking the cause of the racket. Five more minutes of that and the pistons would be shot, the cylinder oil feed blown. No amount of relining would save one of the finest machines on this side of the continent. It was nothing but outright vandalism, and on any other day I would have raced in and laid waste to the operator to stop his vile assault. But none of the nearby guards seemed to take much interest, and on this last day of everything there was no way I was going to stick my neck out for anything but myself.

"Absolutely criminal," I said to no one in particular. This sort of behaviour was all too common when companies announced an end to operations. Years back and not too many myles from here, I had seen a Himmelstein 250 running full tilt with the compressor disconnected and the primary percussion ring filed off. Steam release valves blew and metal ground on metal. The spandrel casings were glowing red-hot, putting the power supply out of reach. I jumped on the machine to pull back on the Wilson force lever, thinking I could salvage the main body of the beast, when twenty laid-off engineers pulled me down and gave me a thrashing I'll never forget.

So let it rust; let it fall to ruin. This time around there was no way I was going to save the world.

I walked up the hill and on over to the pay office. A crowd of men in filthy denims milled around outside, smoke from their cigarettes lingering in a big blue cloud. I went into the lobby. A long line of workers snaked along the walls. The line began at the pay clerk's wicket near the far end of the room. The wicket doors were shut tight. I joined the end of the line near the lobby doors.

The men in line were restless and looked like they had been waiting for some time. Some were telling jokes and others arguing, but otherwise boredom had settled in. Every now and then someone would come into the lobby and try to cut in line, people would shove and shout, and the impudent man would be sent to the back of the line in defeat.

Once every few minutes the pay clerk's wicket would open, the clerk would say something to the men at the front of the line and then slam the doors shut. More shouting would follow from the line.

"What's happening?" I said to the man in front of me. "Are they paying anyone yet?"

"How should I know?" the man said. "I'm only about ten goddamn inches closer to the office than you." The men in front of him laughed.

"That much closer, but not the slightest bit smarter," I said. More laughter.

"You got a goddamn smart mouth, mister," the man said. The ones who had laughed all turned around to see how this would play out. The line-up on either side of us backed away ever so slightly in preparation for the inevitable brawl, but before either one of us could say or do anything, a bigger commotion had blown up further along the line. Someone had tried to cut in and wouldn't be put off by the guys trying to shove him back. A full-scale fistfight had broken out, and things up there were looking pretty serious.

Just then the company security chief barreled out of the clerk's office and ran up to the man who had started the whole ruction. The chief spun the man around and pinned him to the wall with an arm across the neck. With his free hand the company cop fished the man's identity card from his coat pocket, looked at it quickly, took a step back, and slapped the man hard across the face with it. We all stared in silence. The chief slapped the man hard from the opposite direction, and then, with the card clutched in his fist, brought it all down hard on top of the man's head. The man crumpled down to the ground, his face red, his limbs in disarray, and his hair looking like a bewitched barley stack.

"You want a bit of trouble, eh?" the chief said, throwing the man's papers down into his face. "Okay, buddy, if that's what you want, I'll help you find it."

The chief picked the man up and hauled him into the pay clerk's office, slamming the door behind them both. For the next couple of minutes, everyone in line stood stone still as we listened to one of our own being beaten with two seasoned fists.

The office door flew open, and the man was thrown out into the lobby. He gingerly gathered himself up off the floor and staggered to the back of the line. Someone picked up his identity card from the floor and passed it on down to him. The man put it into his coat pocket and hung his head.

"Anyone else want a word with me in the office?" the security chief said, a thick hand hovering over his holstered pistol. No one said anything. He went into the office and shut the door.

After a while, the wicket opened and the clerk began to dole out the last pay packet for the company's workers. In an hour I was face to face with the pay clerk. He looked at my identity card and matched it up with my time sheets. A few calculations, then recalculations, and then he handed me an envelope stuffed with small bills.

I handed Limpy's identity card to the pay clerk.

"What's this?"

"It's Limpy Spence's card. I'm here to get his pay."

"That's against company regulations," the clerk said. From one corner of the office the security chief looked over at me.

"C'mon. Here's his card. Why make a big deal about it?" I said.

"You heard him," the chief said. "Move along."

A man walked out of a manager's office.

"Hey, Joe," I called out.

"Oh, hi, Ed. How's it going?" Joe said. He came over and we shook hands. "Picking up your pay packet?"

"Yup," I said. "And Limpy's, too." I noticed the pay clerk working on Limpy's time sheets. The company cop over in the corner had his face buried in a newspaper.

"Good. Good. Sorry to see it all end," Joe said.

"Yeah, me too."

"Give my best to Limpy."

"Will do," I said, and Joe walked out the front doors.

"Here's Mr. Spence's pay," the clerk said, handing me two small coins.

"What's this?" I said.

"His pay," the clerk said.

"You're joking," I said, handing the coins back.

"Mr. Spence is owed this much in pay," the clerk said, pointing to a figure in his account books. "And these amounts are what we need to deduct from his pay. See? Boots: this amount. Gloves: this amount. Bandages: this amount. Sundries: this amount. Drinking water: this amount down here."

"You've robbed him blind," I said.

"This figure here," he continued, pointing to his account books, "is what the company owes Mr. Spence in wages. And this figure over here is what Mr. Spence owes the company for purchases from the company."

"Do you sleep well?" I said.

"And these coins are the balance in Mr. Spence's favour," the pay clerk said, as he tossed them on the counter in front of me. I put them in my pocket and walked away.

I left the company site for the last time and walked back down the street. I felt again like I did when I left Pete's barbershop, the strength draining from me, and my skin hot with sweat. For one brief moment, I thought the wind was about to pick up all the paving stones to reveal the beach that must lie beneath.

But the wind just carried the dust around in circles.

I pulled a comb from my pocket and tried to sweep my hair back into place. Everywhere men were gathering up what they owned, or going up to get their last pay packet, or wandering around saying good-bye to friends before heading down to the rail station. I walked on.

Punchy's place was still full as I passed. Slowing my pace, I looked in through the window. Punchy was still hustling from table to table, beer and steaks and cigars like manna to everyone inside. Skipper was in there, and I could see Max, as well. The pipe-smoking Scot was over in one corner, as were the Ethiopians: Gideon and Teddy. Some of them sported fresh haircuts, their last from Pete.

I moved on down to my bunkhouse. Limpy was sitting out in front on the curb with our duffel bags beside him. He was leaning forward with an arm outstretched into the street, a long knife in his hand. A large chunk of bread was stuck on the end of the knife, and Limpy waved it at a brawny grey rat. Limpy made little circular turns in the air with the knife, luring the rat in close.

"Go on, little fella," Limpy said, a cigarette bobbing up and down in his lips as he spoke. "Come get your supper."

The giant rat looked at me approaching and took a dive for the bread, snatching it and running as Limpy howled with laughter.

"Goddamn cheeky squirrels, eh?" he said to me.

"Hi, Limpy," I said. "Got everything?"

"Yeah, that's it, Ed."

"Here's your pay," I said, handing him my pay envelope. He took it and looked at the wad of bills inside.

"That's it?" he said.

"Yup," I said, rattling the two coins in my pocket. "Deductions and everything. You know how it is. They sure don't leave you much."

Limpy wiped the long knife on his pant leg. He pulled a tube of Brylcreem from his duffel bag, took the cap off, squeezed a bead of the white gel onto the knife blade, and combed it back along his hair from crown to ducktail, sweeping everything together into solid shape.

"I'm hungry," Limpy said, putting the knife and Brylcreem away. "You want me to get you something?"

"Yeah, why not?" I said. I wasn't really hungry. The day was wearing on me, making me feel empty and sick. But we walked over to a little sidewalk stall where a couple of Arabs with moustaches, cropped black hair, and custom-cut sideburns in the Eaglesmith style were making shawarma. One of them sliced bits of roasted lamb off a grilling spit, while the other gathered up the meat, some chopped tomatoes, and a few spices and rolled it all up in a flat bread. We sat down on the curb to eat our snack. The two Arabs sat beside us, both of them drinking large cups of hot maté.

"What now, Ed?"

"I hear there's some work up north," I said. "We'll be fine,"

Limpy lit a cigarette and ran a hand back through his crashing waves of hair. He seemed thinner, more frail by the minute, as if each breath of the putrid air and each draw on the end of his cigarette served to fuel whatever was making him waste away.

"I know you'll be alright," Limpy said. "I think I'm about done."

I couldn't look at him. "Don't say that. You'll get hired on somewhere just like me."

"You know I got a wife and family, Ed. Maybe I should go home now. There's a good chance they're still there waitin' for me. It's been a long time."

"Maybe," I said. What did I know? There was no place like that I could go back to. I didn't think it likely that any woman I'd know would still be waiting around somewhere for me to come back. There would be no place to return to, just new places where I would try to find work and some small comforts. Places like Punchy's.

"Well, then. Let's go," I said, standing up and brushing crumbs from my pants. "We'll at least walk to the train station together."

"Okay, Ed," Limpy said. We shook the hands of the two Arab cooks, threw the duffel bags over our shoulders, and walked down to the station.

The rail station was packed. Hundreds milled around on the platforms and in the waiting rooms, their worldly goods stacked around them. Porters struggled with all manner of crates and cases through the crowds, pushing their way towards the carriages and boxcars. Two long trains lined both platforms and more sat waiting on the sidings. Engineers, brakemen, and conductors hurried back and forth along the trains making last minute preparations. Quite a large number of men had climbed on top of the rail cars, and no one had done a goddamn thing to stop them.

"I think the one on the far platform is going up the northern line, Limpy," I said. "I better hurry to grab a spot."

"Yeah. This here one'll take me home, Ed."

"Better get going then, or there'll be no room," I said.

We shook hands. Our eyes met for a second. Limpy turned around and in an instant was lost in the swarms boarding the train. I walked back through the crowd and out the main door of the station. I found a place to sit on the front steps. I put a hand in my jacket pocket and rattled the two coins.

Leon Rooke

CONDITIONAL SPHERE OF EVERYDAY HISTORICAL LIFE

In her younger days the woman who would become known as Old Mother had traipsed hither and yon, with never a home. She had come to pal with a gang of rover men, as most beings did at this time, since no other society was known or available to her.

In her ballooning the men shunned her and made her feel herself the outcast slave of them all. But one day a stranger arrived at their campsite. "Our time and being are at slip," he said, "and we must be done with our old split-headed gods who spit nothing but torment and rancour. We must offer our faith to the god of the one head and go forth in the founding of nations." Seated by their fire through the long evening, he endeavoured to set the rover men to thinking right on such issues.

It was at this point that the woman who would become known as Old Mother walked into the firelight, installing a cook-pot above the flames. The stranger teaching the religion of the one-headed god saw her swollen belly and knew then that fortune had steered him to a place of destiny. "Who has seeded this woman?" the man asked, and the men looked away from each other – in consternation at the naiveté of the question – inasmuch as they had as a community conspired in her taking.

"Are you members of the new order of humanity, then," the theologian said, "or shall you continue in the pathways of the alien?" The rovers in the encampment voiced "yea" to the former, for there was much about time and being and their existence under the stars which was disagreeable, as their split-headed gods slaughtered their numbers indiscriminately. They were anxious for something better.

The woman who would become known as Old Mother stirred the pot and fed them, and the stranger studied anew her high belly and the faces of the men who had seeded her.

"Tear off these slithers of tree-bark," he said to them, "and on each slither write your name's symbol, them that can. Them that cannot, then whisper same to me, and I will write down that name. We will put all these names in my hat, and stir the slithers about, and if you trust me I will blindly pluck one from the pot. Whichever slip it is, that will be the woman's name, and the name to be carried by the daughter or son born to her when she sojourns into the future to found our new nation of right and good thinking. "

But the rovers shied from putting their marks into the hat, and stomped and yelled as much as though their old gods of the split heads were again occupying their bodies. The "nations" idea was one foreign to their way of thinking, and how could such a fanciful configuration of beings be managed, and what was the time involved until such a whimsical condition might be realized? If their marks were to be in the hat as fathers of this brave initiative, then what was to be their personal liability if affairs did not go smoothly? Would the vengeful gods of the split heads return to smite or shackle them and drive them away into slavery?

"These are ancient questions unworthy of our release into modernity," the theologian said. "Look ye for the positive function in your existential angst."

The rover men then tried claiming some in their number had been with the woman more than the other and these parties should put their names into the hat by the twenty-fold. They argued on this matter endlessly, as the woman meanwhile swept the clearing for more wood and kept the fire going and bit her lips silent, as she had been compelled to do throughout her own long endurance of all matters pertaining to her time and being. It was a man's world, here among the rovers or elsewhere; fate had yet to decree that she could be in swing with her true and destined orbit.

It was a dreadful cold night, the sky rank and heaving, and the shrubs and tree-limbs nearby their enclosure at glittery freeze.

Eventually one of the rover men agreed he would put his name fifteen times into the hat, since that was his notion of times spent with her, and the others should do likewise, each according to his private reckoning. So they agreed on this method. But they bickered interminably when it came to the particularities of these reckonings, some remembering the one event but denying the other and all confused by those nights when the woman was made to trek from one straw patch to the next, on and on through the night, and by those nights, too, when they were all too wickedly under the influence of fermented juices even to consider with whom she lay or what had been done with her.

The woman busied herself with her tasks, and her opinion on these matters was not germane to anyone's time and being.

In the end the rover men agreed they would together enter forty slips of bark into the hat, plus the fifteen that had already been agreed upon. By this late hour in the proceedings they were all aswell with merriment and filled with self-importance, with food and drink in their gullets to the plenty; thus and so, it came to pass, at the religious fellow's urging, that they consented each to put one gold piece into the hat, for the woman to take away with her that she might provide her offspring with the proper refinements in this new nation of the one god with the one head and not the direful many.

The theologian collected these coins and dropped the mark of their names into his hat. But as he was stirring the names about, one of the men stopped him and said the stranger's mark should be in the hat as well, since he was a good fellow and regular to the bone, and one of them. The other rover men thought this a sound idea, and said furthermore they would make no call of the woman this evening themselves, for they were sick to their guts of her, and she could be his for the taking.

The theologian studied the woman a long time.

"Why have you been beating her?" he asked.

The men denied any whipping of her beyond the normal. They had done by her only what the flesh prescribed as their natural duty. They said she had stumbled upon them all gashed of skin, and that skin rusted, and her hair untamed, and her face swollen this very way he saw it. They reckoned it was how she had come from the harrowing, or how she had aged, or a result of what ill handling other rover gangs had perpetrated upon her, and none of it their doing beyond that which was ordinary and natural.

"How old are you?" the visitor asked the woman.

But he had to shake her by the shoulders and yank at her hair and pry open her mouth with a stick before she replied.

She did not know. And what did it avail her anyway to pursue such knowledge since each day and night of her life had been each day and night alike in its horror?

"Where is it you hail from?"

The fire crackled and the cinders flared and some while passed before she lifted a weary arm and poked it vaguely into the outer dark.

The religious man studied her features some seconds longer, ill at ease with her godless attitude and thinking her undeserving as one who would go now into unknown storms to found the new nation built upon the god of the one head and not the direful many.

He said, "Take up that bowl yonder, and go ye wash yourself."

The rover men hooted and clapped their visitor about the shoulders, so aroused were they by his many strange notions, such as this one called washing.

The religious man spat on a blackened stick pulled from the fire and wrote the mark of his name down the once, and dropped his own slither of bark into the hat. He spun the names about, and pulled one out, reciting it aloud to the group – and this was thus the name the woman later to be known as Old Mother that evening took as her own, which would also, of course, become known as the name of the founded country under the god of the one head and not the direful many.

During the night, the theologian's cold legs at last at rest between the woman's own, she clutched the gold pieces in tight fists to her chest, and the slither of bark bearing the name tight in one fist as well. There were not but the seven gold pieces, though the men who had had their way with her in this camp were many more in number, which did not seem to her to be right.

She wondered which one of the rover gang bore this frightful name, and what that name signified for her future on this planet where time and being were alike as one in its horror.

"How does a mouth say this name?" she asked the visitor during the night, after he had awakened and had his rough way with her a second time.

The man uttered a word, then a stream of words, each perplexing to her ears – strange words such as fearful animals might speak when issuing warnings to each other through dark nights.

They were not sounds which conveyed anything to her, nor any her tongue could easily wrap around. They were not any of them a sound heard these loathsome months she'd been urchin-slave to this crew of motley rovers. She wondered it was not the religious man's name, him whose eyes were lit with a passion for the ringed heavens but whose hands had been as coarse as a rover's.

Most likely, she thought, these were names pumped up out of the very air, with no attachment to either time or being.

Afterwards, she saw him rooting in the dirt and among the rags of their clothing, doubtlessly in search of the seven gold coins. But in a while he tired of this, and tired of beating her, and returned to profound sleep.

They were an evil brew, these men, but at least they had done right by her in the end, giving her these legal names under invocation of the new theology.

In the morning, long before first light, the woman struck off, darting fearful glances back at the sordid camp to see if any would come chasing after her, to catch her hair and drag her back, as had been her ill luck so often in the past.

She pressed on through the frozen shadows.

She hoped both to the god of the one head and to the split-many that the chosen name would be a name to bring fortune's good breath to the strange being unaccountably at roost inside her body.

Whatever else was to follow from that news was a matter beyond all conjecture.

Before quitting the encampment she had seen the religious man skip warily off into darkness. She had witnessed a new gang of bedraggled rover men creep in with stone and spear, and heard the gods of the split heads and the one-headed god at warfare, all howling without mercy.

In no way, to her mind, could a god of the single head defeat innumerable gods whose smoking bodies were affixed with the direful many.

Whether man or gods, someone would follow.

She took to water.

As daylight arrived, she saw in the sky a swooping eagle. Later, she saw the bird a second time, and in the evening, when she rested, she saw it yet again, looking down on her from a tree's high bough.

Carry me along, dark flier was her peculiar thought.

Soon enough, her way strewn by the rubble of malignant gods of the one head and the many, she had reached new lands that in later ages of time and being would be affixed with a score of unpronounceable names. Just as she, by that ageless scoring, was already known as Old Mother. Her many children and their descendants had been swept hither and yon as though by hurricane, imparting their own names to this and the other unhewn country.

We were each of us by that hour at swim with romance and mystery.

Helen Marshall

LESSONS IN
THE RAISING OF
HOUSEHOLD
OBJECTS

Mummy asks me how I am doing, and I tell her that I am afraid of the twins.

This is true. I don't know who the twins are. In fact, the twins aren't anybody yet. In fact, the twins are quite probably dead. Mummy tells me I don't really know what dead means, but I most certainly do know what dead means. When Scamper forgot how to wag his tail on my third birthday, Daddy told me that meant that he had died, and I said "oh," and he said, "So now you know what dead means, that's good, that's good, sweetheart, you're growing up." So I do know what dead means; it means when you stop being what you were before.

Mummy doesn't like that I am afraid of the twins.

Mummy insists that I press my head up against her belly until her little poked-out belly button fits right into my ear. It feels strange there, but it also feels normal, as if belly buttons were designed for ears.

Then there is a kick, and then there is another, and I know that the twins are mad at me, so I start to cry. I don't like crying very much but sometimes you can't really help crying. It's just something you have to do.

Mummy pats me on the back and she says. "It's okay, darling, honey, peanut, Miss Angela Clothespin Jacket." My real name is Angela Chloe Jackson, but I like that other name for me better even though it isn't real.

"I don't want them, I want them to stay there, I don't want them to come out," I tell her, but I am still crying so she doesn't hear me. The thing about Mummys is that they can't hear what you're saying whenever you are crying, and so I hate crying, but like I already said, sometimes it's just what happens.

But, anyway, that isn't quite what I meant because I don't want them to stay there. I don't want them to stay anywhere, but maybe inside Mummy is better than outside Mummy where they will have to roll around with their lumpy flesh and the tangled-up arms and legs like Daddy showed me in the black and white picture.

Mummy says, "But Angie, Mummy's tummy will get too big. They can't stay in there forever."

And I think, yes, that is exactly the problem.

❧

I decide that I will be a good little girl, and I will practice loving the twins.

Mummy says it is important that I love them and that I am nice to them because they will be very fragile when they come out. "Like a lamp?" I ask. I have broken the lamp in my room more than once, and then I have to sleep in the dark because of it so that I will learn. Daddy calls this an object lesson.

And Daddy says, "Like the lamp except even more fragile than that."

"If you're very good," Mummy says, "I'll let you hold them." I wonder what it will be like to hold those things.

"But what if I break them?" I ask, and Mummy just purses her lips in that way and says, "You'll have to be very careful, Angie."

Mummy asks, "Do you want to feel them kick again?" and I say, "No," because how can you love something that is trying to kick you? I must practice first on something easier to love than the twins.

I find two cans of tomato soup in the pantry because tomato soup is the thing I like most, specially with toasted cheese. Tomato soup will be easy to love. Even without the toasted cheese.

I am not supposed to go in the pantry by myself, but I think Mummy and Daddy will like it if I learn how to love the twins so I do even though it is dark and I am worried about the shelves and all the other things there are in the dark.

I name one of the cans Campbell. I name the other Simon because I cannot name both of them Campbell. I decide that Campbell must be the older of them, but I think, deep down, that I like Simon better. He is better behaved. And besides, he doesn't have any dents. His label is crisp and new.

Campbell and Simon must stay with me if I am to learn how to love them. Sometimes I watch them. They are not very interesting to watch. I decide that it is probably because Simon is too well behaved, and so I love him a little bit less for that. I try rolling Campbell down the stairs. Afterward, he is slightly more dented than he was before, and I decide that this is what Daddy calls an object lesson. Simon says nothing.

"You're supposed to say something, Simon," I tell him. "You shouldn't let me roll Campbell down the stairs, not if he's a baby." And Simon starts to cry so I can't hear what he's saying, and I decide that I don't love him at all. I tell him I like cream of broccoli better. I tell him I like chicken with noodles, and why couldn't he be chicken with noodles? Simon is crying even more now, but that's what babies do. They don't ever say anything, they just cry.

Finally, I give Simon to Mummy who always helps me when I am crying. Later on, Mummy gives me tomato soup and toasted cheese for lunch. I look at Campbell with his dented rim and his sad, sad face. I hope that this has been an object lesson for him.

≈✺≈

The problem is that Mummy is not getting bigger because the twins are getting bigger, but Mummy is getting bigger because the twins are thieves.

The morning that Mummy came home and said to me, "Darling, baby girl, Angela C., you're going to have brothers!" was the first time I knew they were thieves. She was smiling so much that her face looked like another person's face, and Daddy's face looked like another Daddy's face, and both of them were hugging each other and hugging me. But after all the hugging was over with, I noticed that my hairbrush was missing, the one with the pink handle that I have used since I was a baby even though it is too small for me because it never hurts. "No," Mummy tells me, "it wasn't the twins," but I know it was, anyway.

≈✺≈

I have come to a decision about Campbell. Well, we have reached the decision together.

The decision is that I will not eat anymore tomato soup because Campbell says it is cruel, and Campbell will help me to catch the twins, who have now carried off not only my hairbrush but also my flower fairy which I only left out to see if she would like the rain, and also the bunny-eared hat that I was given at Christmas. I do not mind losing the flower fairy and the hat so much but that was a really good hairbrush and Mummy says they don't make them anymore, so now I have to use a grown-up hairbrush, and grown-up hairbrushes pull and pull and pull until I am crying all over again.

So I will leave Campbell out on the bookshelf next to my bed, and I will keep on the night lamp so that he can see properly even though I am now fully too old for it, and night lamps are stupid anyway, but Campbell gets scared of the dark and besides, how else will he see the twins?

Mummy and Daddy come and kiss me goodnight, and Daddy smells wonderful, like cinnamon and coffee and chocolate, but Mummy doesn't smell like Mummy at all. When she sits on my bed I can feel it moving as the twins go kick, kick, kick. I think to myself, or rather, I say to Campbell, "Look, you can see them kicking, just you wait and see." But Mummy doesn't like it when I talk to Campbell, and Daddy has to say, "No, honey, it's okay, we won't take Campbell away," and then I stop crying.

In the morning, Campbell is sitting in exactly the same place, and my stuffed Adie is gone, who I liked best because one eye was blue and one eye was green and dogs don't normally look like that.

"Campbell," I say, but Campbell is still asleep and so he doesn't answer me.

❧

This is how the twins come out, I think.

There is a hole in Mummy's tummy. I have seen it because that's what the belly button keeps all plugged up, and that's why her belly button points out now, because the twins are pushing on the other side. At night, when Mummy is under her covers, I think she cannot see her belly button anymore and, anyway, just like Campbell she has to fall asleep. That is when the twins come out. Daddy says that the twins are still quite small so I think they must be able to still fit in through the belly button.

Sometimes when I am sleeping I hear noises. I think it must be the twins and I want to say to them, "Go back inside! You're supposed to be dead still!" But I don't think they can hear me very well. Maybe that is because I am whispering it to Campbell.

It is scary when the twins are outside of Mummy and sometimes I have to hold Campbell very close to me. I don't love him just yet, but I think I might be somewhere close to loving him. I say it is okay if he falls asleep and he says that he loves me very much.

"They are taking things, I know they are," I whisper to Campbell and we are both afraid together. In the morning things are a little bit different than they were the night before and Mummy's tummy is a little bit bigger. I think they must be building a tent inside, filling Mummy up with hairbrushes and flower fairies and bunny-eared hats and Adie.

The next time Mummy asks me to listen to the twins, I put my ear against her tummy. I think I feel the shape of the hairbrush and I think I can hear Adie barking, so I bite Mummy's belly button until there is blood, because if I can get in then maybe I can get them back. Now Mummy is crying though, and so I can't understand what she is saying, and Daddy is so mad that he puts me in my room and he turns out the light and he takes away the night lamp and he takes away Campbell.

So now I am sitting in the darkness, and I have the blankets close to me and I miss Campbell, which makes me think I must be starting to love him a little, but I am also thinking that this must be what it is like for the twins inside Mummy's tummy.

❧

I don't know where Campbell is, and when I go into the cupboard there are other cans of soup, but they aren't Campbell and so I cannot love them.

I wonder if maybe the twins have taken Campbell too, or if maybe they are in cahoots with Mummy and Daddy.

"Mummy," I say, when she opens the door at last and is standing in the doorway and there is light all around her so that it hurts my eyes. "Is Campbell inside you?" I ask, but she just squeezes her lips until they aren't lips anymore, they are just a single line that she cannot speak out of, and then she closes the door again.

✤

I am trying not to think about Campbell anymore. I am trying to pretend that there has never been a Campbell, and so in the morning I eat cereal and I think to myself, that this tastes nothing like tomato soup and that is a good thing.

Mummy is still hugging Daddy, but neither of them wants to look at me properly so I just eat my cereal. I pretend that I can't see Mummy's tummy moving when the twins kick. But I am thinking to myself, *I know that you are in there, I know that you are all in there,* and Mummy has no idea that I can see all of the things that are starting to poke out of her, because she is not big enough for all the special sequined purses and shoe racks and televisions and night lamps and Adies and bunny-eared hats and flower fairies and Campbells that she has inside of her. There, right there, I can see the spokes of my brand new ten-speed bicycle poking out of her, but she has no idea and neither does Daddy when he hugs her.

⊸✠⊷

I don't know how the twins have done it but they have taken Daddy too.

Last night he was here and kissed me on the forehead and he read from my special book, the only book that is left now, and he said, "Where are your other books, Angie?" and I said, "The twins have taken them, Daddy." Then he touched my forehead very lightly like a butterfly, and said, "You can't keep doing this, honey, peanut, darling. The twins are coming and they are coming soon."

Daddy doesn't understand, but now Daddy has gone too, and I am afraid he is deep inside Mummy and we won't be able to get him out.

But I have a plan.

This is my plan. I will lay a trap for the twins. I will catch the twins and then maybe I will be able to give them what Daddy calls an object lesson so they will know that they can't keep doing this anymore.

❧

I don't have a night lamp and I don't have Campbell and I don't have Daddy, so I must do this alone.

I take my special book, the one book that I have left, and I tie a string around it just like Daddy taught me to tie my shoelaces, and then I tie another string around my wrist because then, even if I fall asleep, I will be able to catch them. Mummy kisses me on the forehead and she asks if I want her to read to me but I shake my head and say, "No, Mummy, I am too old for reading," because being too old is when things stop working the way they did before. So Mummy smoothes my hair like she did when I was itsy bitsy, and she sits on the bed with me. I want to tell her not to sit on the bed, that I don't want the twins that close to me, but Mummy is so big with all the dish-washers and book shelves and staircases and base-ments sticking out of her that I can't believe she even fits on the bed.

"Are they building a house in there, Mummy?" I ask, and Mummy just laughs and shakes her head. "No, Angela Clothespin Jacket, they are not building a house, they are going to come live in our house."

Then I am crying again, and I cry until I go to sleep.

❧

I wake up in the middle of the night and there is a tugging at my wrist, so I look at my wrist and there is the string, and the string is pulled out all the way to the book and then there is the twins. The twins are not two people, they are just one person, and they are not a person at all because, really, they are just a bunch of arms, and legs, and foreheads like in the picture.

"Why don't you just go away?" I ask the twins. And the twins say, "Because we love you, Angela Clothespin Jacket. You know what it is like to live in the dark, just like we do. We want you to come live with us forever inside Mummy where it is safe and warm and there are night lamps and there is Campbell and Adie." I think about this for a while because I don't like the twins very much, but it is lonely out here and perhaps it will be less lonely inside Mummy, in the dark, with the twins. At least then we will be all together, even if it is inside Mummy.

I say, "Okay, twins," and then I go through the belly button with them.

❧

The thing is that the twins are cleverer than I thought.

Adie is in here and Campbell too, and the flower fairy, but the twins have locked the belly button and it is very dark and I don't know how to get out.

I feel around, amidst the ten-speed bikes and the sequined purses and the night lamps, and then there is a sound and it is Daddy. I am feeling very scared, so I climb over the bookshelf and the club chair until there he is, smelling like cinnamon and coffee and chocolate. I want him to hold me, but it is too crowded for holding in here.

"They are out there," I say to Daddy. "The twins are out there."

And he says, "Yes, peanut, honey, darling, the twins are out there, but that is where they are supposed to be. That's the way Mummy wanted it to be."

Daddy cannot hold me, so I hug Campbell close to me because he is small enough for holding.

"We have made some bad decisions," I say to Daddy, and he says, "No, peanut, this is what was supposed to happen. This is what we planned for all along, it was supposed to be the twins coming out and you going back in."

"Why?" I ask Daddy. "Because," he says, "we wanted a baby who didn't cry as much. We wanted a baby who didn't have so many names as you. We wanted a baby who was real."

"I can be a real baby," I say. Maybe I say that. I'm crying, so it is difficult to tell.

"No, honey, that's not the way it works. That's why I'm down here. Now that the twins are born you have to live here forever. This is your new room."

"Inside Mummy?" I ask.

"Yes, peanut, inside Mummy, with all the other things we don't need anymore."

I think about this for a while. I cannot see Daddy's face in the darkness. All I can smell is cinnamon and coffee and chocolate, and I decide that I don't like those things anymore. Those are just things, and they aren't Daddy.

"No," I say to Daddy, "I'm going to get out of here, and when I do I'm not going to take you with me."

Daddy doesn't like this very much, but I don't care. I like this, and Campbell likes this, so I think we will be okay.

◦✖◦

It is time for another plan, I say to Campbell, and Campbell also thinks it is time for another plan.

I take Campbell and I put him in Mummy's sequined purse and I put it over my shoulder. Then I climb the bookshelf and feel along the top of Mummy's tummy, which is big and curved like being underneath an umbrella. Daddy tells me to stop doing that but I have decided that I will not listen to Daddy anymore. I know that there is a belly button somewhere and so all I have to do is find it.

"You can't do that," says Daddy. "Someone must stay in here to mind the house and it won't be me!"

"Well, Daddy," I say, "you should have thought about that before you came in here."

I climb from the bookshelf to the club chair to the minivan, and for a moment I wonder how on earth the twins managed to fit all of these things inside Mummy, but then I stop wondering and I keep climbing. Finally, I discover the belly button at the very top of Mummy's tummy.

I put my ear to the belly button, and I can hear that on the outside Mummy is laughing. I think she must be laughing because the twins are doing something funny like telling jokes or aerial acrobats, and I hate the twins a little bit more for making Mummy laugh, and I hate Mummy a bit more for loving the twins like that. But at least I have Campbell, and at least Daddy has already taught me how to tie and untie knots.

I start to untie the belly button, and Daddy says to me, "You'll never be able to get out there, you're not a real daughter, Miss Peanut, Miss Honey, you're not a real Angela, you're just clothespins and jackets."

"No," I say to him, "I am too real. You made me because you wanted me and so I am as real as the twins and I am real as Campbell, and we are getting out of here right this very instant!"

First there is a light, and my eyes hurt because I have gotten used to the dark, but Campbell tells me to be brave, that it will be okay out there, and I say, "I love you, Campbell." He says, "I love you, baby girl," and I like it when Campbell calls me that, so I tug at the string and the light gets brighter and the hole gets bigger. Then I am sticking my head out and then I am staring at Mummy and she is staring at me, and I am half inside her and half outside of her so I climb out the rest of the way even though I can hear Daddy crying still from inside.

"What are you doing here?" she asks.

"I just wanted to see the sunshine," I say. And there are the twins, and they are all the things that they were before but somehow they look more and more like people and the people they look like are Mummy and Daddy. But when I look at Mummy, Mummy looks more and more like just a mess of arms and legs and skirts and pantyhose and lipstick and eyelashes and not the thing that she was before.

"Are you going to stay?" she asks me.

"Yes," say the twins, "please stay with us, Angela Clothespin Jacket! We can all be real babies together! It would be good to have a sister!"

I think about this for a bit because maybe I want to stay with Mummy and Daddy and the twins. Maybe I want to be with them, even though none of us are the things we were before. But then I take

Campbell out of the purse and he whispers something in my ear.

"This has been a real object lesson," I say to Mummy, and I am holding Campbell close to my chest because I love him so very much, "but I think we will be going now."

And we do.

Priscila Uppal

COVER BEFORE STRIKING

The most common phrase in the world in print is Cover Before Striking. Thousands of books with tiny cardboard flaps in every language telling the same story, the same lie. It's madness to think with all the warnings, no one seems to be listening.

every language telling the same story

Crazy was a word my father used a lot, especially in association with women. Women were invented to create havoc for men, my father said. Fire-eaters. Looking to cause trouble where there doesn't need to be any. Set fire to your pants and then to your house. That's what women do. You would nod and make faces. I would say nothing, until later, in my bed, when he would rub my belly and ask those questions. I would have to answer. Crazy. Irrational, if he felt like being more psychological about it. Those things never happened. You made them up. You're always telling stories. You are lying.

a word my father used a lot

Lying crazy on your living room floor. Burgundy carpet burned, frayed, pink spots from vodka spills, keeps my back warm, tickled, like fur on my knees. Yellow plastic ashtray bought at the discount store in the market, Made in Taiwan. You laughed and said we were all Made in Taiwan. And I imagined myself being melted into a shape with grooves for sticks and fingers to fit. With small black type across my back and ashes smeared on my face. Watch the smoke curl and rise like runaway clouds in a storm, afraid of catching the fever, paper burning in staircase spirals the way I thought fairy tale houses would, filter glowing like a pulsating wound, flicking my lighter on and off, on and off, each crack from my fingertips making me tremble. Intoxication. Your feet dangle over my hair, wide and black spread on red. Yellow light telling me to slow down. Slow down. The dizzy feeling in my belly, the downtown traffic. Gazing at the ceiling, dripping the last swig of vodka onto my thighs to mix with your come. My grooves sore but aching for your fingers. I am lost in the smoke.

curl and rise like runaway clouds

He would smile when he said it. Dark thinning hair without a part. Bushy eyebrows furled in amusement. Lips a tense bow. Arms like pendulums. I never knew which side he was going to take. Swing. Swing. I wanted to hit him. Make the movement stop. Take his balding head in my shaking hands and beat it on our yellow fridge, watch the magnets (mushroom, doctor's number, pizza place, pre-school blushing heart), watch them fall to the floor like exploding stars and the picture I had drawn three years earlier, still up on the fridge because no one paid attention, curled at the corners, smudged with fingerprints, grease from cooking, frying our food always in too much oil. Everything we ate in shades of brown or black, burnt bread and fried, trying to disguise the smell with fans whirling, whirling smoke and ashes all over the kitchen, beating the alarm with a broom handle to stop the wailing, wailing, announcing our food was overcooked, overdone, again. Stashing the broom in the crack between the fridge and cupboard. I wanted that lilac to fall. All other flowers wilt. I wanted to press his face up against it, beat him with the broom handle I'd felt on my back, my back, and lower than that. Make him bleed. See I was still a child three years ago drawing with crayolas, sometimes unable to stay inside the lines.

all other flowers wilt

Dinnertime. I am tired of mashed potatoes and peas, green and white mush served in sterile silence. Only sometimes a smile from the pretty nurse, the one with long raven-black hair feathered like crows' wings, brushed back into a silver pin that glitters under the blinds. I want to feel her hair and have her feed me with her large spoon like a child. I usually accept another helping to watch her move, row by row. I know I could've been a nurse like her. I like to think she could've been me.

Dinnertime

Smile, you said. You're such a sorry drunk. Good fuck considering, but stop being so sad. And don't look up at me like that. You know it's true. Show me your tits. Come on. I'm just teasing. Have another beer. Take a toke. I got more. We can get more if you want. Just stop lying there being sad. We could play a game. We could get under those covers again. We could smoke up more afterwards. What do you think? What game would you like to play this time?

don't look up at me like that

We played the thermostat game daily. Behind your eyes I'd sneak and sweat, aware of your body lying somewhere on the other side of the wall, risking getting caught to see if we could steal more heat. Hiding in blankets. Rolling ourselves into balls. Breathing into each other's hands. It never felt warmer but the rising thermometer told me I'd won. I'd stolen something from you. It was enough.

aware of your body lying somewhere

12 was not as attractive as 13. 13 wasn't quite as sophisti-
cated as 14. And 16 was where I wanted to be kissing boys
in alleys, getting felt up. Until of course 18 when you've done
all that and it's old hat. Childish. You are beginning to do it
well now, with rhythm. You know what makes you feel up
instead of being felt up.

16 was where I wanted to be

Up there, he said, pointing with his skinny arms to the planet he is going to save. Up is where you go when you die. Past the airplanes and the clouds. That's why I'm going to save it. Past the moon? I asked. Past everything. This house. This street. Your school. You get to get out of here and play. I am going to be a hero. I thought my brother was very wise. Will you take me with you? I asked.

Up is where you go when

The telephone was black with white numbers, the rotary kind that clicked while the dial spun, plotting each number like Morse code. Click, click, click. Under the door I barred with my dresser and rocking chair, feet hooked to the vent. My huge wooden dresser with the white lamb painted on the drawers. Tiny balloon labels to proclaim what was inside. Miscellaneous on the one that kept my writings, aligning myself with knickknacks and old candy wrappers, yelling that I was calling Children's Aid. I saw it as a flashing red siren sign like the ones in front of hospitals and emergency medical clinics, ambulances and fire trucks roaring in, a large man sweeping me up in his arms and carrying me off like a baby down a long white ladder as flames flew out the windows, fireworks exploding on the lawn, the man cradling my limbs and singing me a lullaby, telling me to fall asleep, asleep, the red truck crying with me, saying I wasn't going crazy, I would be OK, I would never have to see the house again. You yelling back that you didn't care. They would never believe a nine, ten, twelve-year-old girl over her own father. They would know I was just a wacko, troublemaker, fire-eater, slut seeking attention. They'd take a picture so they'd have my number next time around and bring me right back. Knuckles in mid-dial, I'd put down the receiver, believing you. You were so large and strong telling me no one else would take care of me. I'd move the furniture, crawl back into bed, and cry, once again, for forgiveness.

Click, click, click

It is too quiet here. My men parading around, bumping into me, moody, moody men roaming inside of me. Waking up, making breakfasts, on the phone, in the shower, moving the pictures around, rearranging the cupboards. Where did you go? Why have you returned to live here, mute and waving? Why do you screech in my ears only when I'm trying to sleep? When I am wanting to wish you good night?

My men parading around, bumping

Take me back to the old neighbourhood, tired bungalows all lined up like cigarettes in a pack, the smell of tarred driveways, the crooked street sign. Ashbrook Crescent. No brook, no pond, just a long curvy street with children playing road hockey, me with my arm in another cast on the sidelines saving worms from the grates and the tires, moving them into camps, slime-covered fingers, the autumn leaves raked into piles to be swept away, dumped into the garbage, even though everyone thinks they're pretty before they fall. Every year the dumpster would catch fire and we would gather around broken gravel and watch the huge green box glow like an abandoned planet, the thick fumes of burnt leaves rustling over the streets, confetti in red, black, yellow, green, dripping and rising in the wind, landing to be buried in a new place, secret messages scattered along the highways and boulevards and our crescent too, forgotten and crumpled, unread, burning. Car, the kids wail and join me on the sidewalk for a few seconds then back to the game. Jersey sweatshirts, hats, belonging to a team, a city, the world, much more than this Ashbrook Crescent without so much as a fire hydrant.

join me on the sidewalk for a few seconds

You wouldn't let me light your cigarettes anymore. I burnt your eyebrows. I missed your eyes.

I burnt your eyebrows

Pyromaniac. I loved the word when I first heard it. Elated when the doctor told me that's what I was. Finally I know. Heat and smoke, the stench of ash, hypnotic effect of light caught in a pure bursting bubble of destruction. This is me. This is who I love. If you don't stop, they will put you away. Put you in a new place. Re-place you. Maniacs are easy to find.

the doctor told me that's what I was

I poured lighter fluid from the Zippo all over them. I didn't want to see the stains from my blood, crusty red rusty reminders of you, sex, the thick smell like fog, if you turn it's overwhelming, your sweat and mine in patches, spills, on the bedsheets, the pinstriped blue sheets. I burned them all. They found me passed out, drunk, matches clasped to my hands, ashes rubbed over my limbs. Man's first invention.

your sweat and mine in patches

You came home without taking a shower. Did you think I couldn't smell her sex on your face as you brushed by to make coffee? It didn't smell like your waitress friend. The redhead with the long fake fingernails, a broken one I found in your suit pocket. A new one. A replacement. My body cold and frigid to your touch. Evenings spent picturing you undressing her. Slow. Calculating. Silk black stockings slipping off like drops of water down a glass, hanging from a chair as you pound into her. Hard and hungry. Your body I know, I can read as Braille, each indentation marking spaces where you live and breathe without me. No more grooves. No more fingers. No more. I'd wonder if your body moved the same way it did with me. First slow like a reptile, scaly and slick, and then quicker, forceful, until you'd bite the side of my armpit and come, your head, neck stretched, past me on the bed, past all of me, holding out for that moment of release, collapsing sweat wet kisses in my hair, holding you like a child at my breast, my thighs red, rough red, red. Did she do that for you? Did she do more? I never asked. I only know her by the smell and the guilty look in your eyes.

like a child at my breast, my thighs

Colours, colours, all the beautiful colours, hues pure, pure, like fireworks, green, yellow, purple, blue pages burnt and blowing away, up, up, up, my diary destroying itself, taking back all those words, all those lies.

all the beautiful colours

They like it when I write here. They don't read it of course. But they like my hands to be busy. They always want to see where our hands are.

when I write here. They don't

My favourite memory of you. One night I broke like the thermostat and couldn't stop melting, though I was cold, cold. Holding my knees, rocking back and forth in the apartment, the television wouldn't stop blinking, my moody men trapped inside reporting the news, solving crimes, waking the dead. Stop, I cried. Stop it right now. You got out the thick camping blanket, the red-and-black plaid one, and wrapped me up. You carried me outside to the patch of grass by the parking garage. The stars fled, I said. You just can't see them, you said. But they're there. Straddling me gently from behind, holding a glass of water to my lips, kissing my hair. Imagine you're a star, you said, even if no one else can see you. You named a constellation after me, arms encircling me like the Milky Way.

holding my knees, rocking back and forth

I learned a soaked pack of matches can be revived if let alone on a sunny day. Though they only spark for a split second. A small atomic bomb.

if let alone on a sunny day

You end all our conversations Take Care. I have been father. I always did and now 400 miles between us you want to check up on me, make sure I'm healthy and happy, not thinking too much or playing with matches, your voice getting shakier as you age. You speak of infections and pills, the nurses, the other men in the home, how you beat them all at chess, such a fine mind you still possess. We tell each other nothing. Nothing we really want to say, like the time you let me cuddle up beside you on the couch and you sang nursery rhymes to me, low monotone voice, inelegant but comforting, black sheep and cockleshells, plums and kidney pies, to put me to sleep, and how you let me win when we arm wrestled and I would prance around, my arms clenched in fists high, high over my head, Champion of Arm Wrestling of the World. And how it changed. You found out I kissed a boy in the school clothes closet and you beat me so bad I couldn't walk for days, my guilty lips broken open and chapped, you told my teacher I'd fallen out of a tree. We tell lies, pretend it's all forgotten. Talk about the weather. And sometimes it seems so far away it shouldn't matter anymore and other times the tension in the cord is so electric it is too much for me to bear. Take Care.

arms clenched in fists high

Hang on tight now, and we raced down the hill, my bum bumping on the bicycle seat, the wind stinging my eyes, yelling with delight, go faster, faster, my arms around your waist, go faster, faster, past all the houses, past the cemetery, so fast until we're actually going backwards, back in time, my hair like a kite in the wind, go faster, faster, I know you can, brother, faster, look back for an instant to wave at those we've left behind.

past all the houses, past the cemetery

Every book of matches has its own story. Date, time, place of purchase, or where I had taken, stolen them from, from whom, and finally what I destroyed neatly labelled on top of the sandpaper striking strip. It was all premeditated. I spoke in tongues. I spoke in tongues.

what I destroyed neatly labelled

I look behind, hearing the sirens, the red trucks arriving, skidding, making no stops, forcing traffic to the sides, men in yellow suits and thick boots like astronauts, holding on at the turn, jumping off, me on the sidewalk watching the smoke rise in black rings into the sky, knowing I was done, I had done it, the frames, ledges, breaking off, falling into pieces, the nosy neighbours leaning out their windows, on the driveway wrapped in winter coats, gawking in gossip horror, on the horn to tell friends about the spectacle, the little girl jumping up and down in the street watching her house burn down, the men running around with their hoses, calling out codes, suited with masks and rubber for protection.

holding on at the turn

Every match a possibility. Every attraction a destruction.

Every

Why? I didn't want to ask him. I didn't know how to put it on. I don't know. You shaking your head, me embarrassed that my brother was the only one I could go to and did he know who. Waiting for the test to finish, in the bathroom, biting nails and then the relief. That I didn't bring another part of me here. Or another part of him.

my brother was the only one

I lit the match. Waiting until my fingertips were so hot they were nearly pokers, curling my lips into a kiss and blowing. Wishing the joy wasn't snuffed out so quickly. My fingers snapping open another match.

snapping open another match

When the fire alarm goes off here, they all turn towards me. Some start screaming or crying, some don't even blink. The orderlies check if they should bother to take us outside or if it is just a false alarm. There hasn't been a real fire since I arrived. When the alarm goes off though, it is the only time I feel at home.

they all turn towards me

Why do you pronounce fire, fear? you asked once.

you asked

I'm radioactive tonight, you said, and left me yelling your name, standing in the rain. You move so much faster than me, up the street in your long lanky strides, you didn't want to hurt me. Lost like a magician in a puff of smoke. You knowing I hate it when you disappear. Hate crying in public, talking to myself to figure out what's wrong, what voices are speaking to you, if they include mine. Radioactive man, burning me with invisible rays, will you return? There are still planets to save.

you didn't want to hurt me. Lost

If he loves you, you've won. You're worth something. More than those girls in nylon mini skirts, neon wallflowers at the clubs, scouting for men without rings, or with them if they're successful enough to set you up. Dabbing at your makeup, making passes into mirrors, moving your body to the music to show your rhythms, how your hips can grind, you can make your tits look bigger with the proper bra, or wear none so your nipples stand out under the lights like stars. But if you love him, get ready to make excuses. Because you're working on it. Making it work out. Working on it even if it's so broke it ain't worth holding together with bubble gum and paper clips. If you work on it, it's serious business. Take this love thing and twist it into a box you can fit into. Even if you're just the corner. Even if you're just the lid.

take this love thing

I would have told you but I wasn't sure how my voice would sound, if it would shake and waver like an expiring flame, falter, make me look guilty, like I was lying. Fire-eater. So I stayed silent, my lips drawn and shut like curtains, you couldn't even guess what was inside the grooves, whose fingers left burn marks on my knees. I didn't want your stories of the clouds and moon to change so I left you and crawled up the chimney.

stories of the clouds and moon

My mind is too full. The nurses look at me with pity or amusement, I'm not always sure which, my pen scratching wildly on diary pages. Some of you are speaking openly and some of you are so silent I'm beating the words out of you.

pity or amusement

My chest hurts. I can't move my right arm. All the faces and voices flitting around like shadows. You running beside me, calling my name over and over, bending your face into me, keeping up with the speed of the stretcher pushed by four pairs of hands. Lips hot. Cracked. Tears in my mouth. I've done it. Again. Couldn't help it. Lost all feeling in my legs, pressing into the mattress. Sirens singing. A lot of talk. Words. I don't understand. Critical condition. You allowed to come. Drape a blanket. Chin tucks down. I try to wiggle my toes. Shock. You can barely look. I'm sorry. I'm sorry.

A lot of talk

Quiet. They make sure of that. So quiet that my head is a medium where ghosts speak. All my moody men running around now packing suitcases, saying goodbye, slipping through the door and the vents, seeping out of my lungs, ashes on their limbs and eyes, a metronome ticking away over my bed so I know when to eat, when to sleep, when to... The calendar so I know when I will have visitors. When you are here, sitting beside me, I show you diaries and you nod your head and smile and sometimes walk to the barred windows to look at the pretty synthetic garden and I know you feel like crying but you won't in front of me. This is your duty. See my burnt, twisted hands, red and scarred, as I struggle to grip a spoon or pen. You have another lover and I don't blame you. I enjoy your visits even though I sit straight, immaculately controlled in front of you. Once in a while you sneak me a cigarette. Of course you light it for me and tuck the matches tightly away in your wallet. I sit by the lilac painting as if all the fire is gone from me.

my head is a medium where ghosts

Brother, you stopped telling me stories about the world beyond the skies and stars. I guess we aren't children anymore. I guess we both got out somehow though you never did pedal fast enough to leave, only fast enough not to stop or skid. I still dream of being wrapped around you like a fall jacket and beating the wind and the roads in a ten-speed race. I dream of your olive skin and long bony legs and the way you held a hockey stick like a magic wand and skated circles around me and I giggled in delight to be the centre of the rink so you could pretend you were flying on silver lightning. I dream of your voice, and how I would think you were a hero disguised in blue jeans and a cotton T-shirt who knew all the stories I could never tell.

I dream of your olive skin and long bony legs

A winter fire actually lasts longer than a summer one. It has something to prove.

actually

If I just get it all out, they say I may find some peace. I am trying to let the memories go, give them away to unseen visitors who may be listening outside the locked doors or behind serving trays or dancing on my windowsill lighting fires under my feet. These are my offerings. My limbs. My candles.

get it all out, they say

You aren't coming next week. My calendar is filled less and less with red marker. Months go by. You are restless and moody. You want to move on. Your arm just there, near the edge of my chair. I could touch it if I tried. I could touch you, your crow-eyed face, and let you know how I cared and maybe let you take me on the bed like you used to, crawling over me, my legs spreading for you to smell and taste, for you to look up at me with hazy eyes, feel me tremble and quiver, kiss you long and hard, all tongues and wet, give this body something to dream about, to smell the sheets later, full of our come and lick them trying to retrieve you. I can't quite make my hand move over to you. Could you touch me? Could you tempt me to dance? Before signing out at the desk could you brush my hair or trace my neck with your lips just one last time?

Could you touch me?

YAKOS SPILIOTOPOULOS

BLACK SHEEP

Lefteri traces the veins along his forearm with the blade-tip of his grandfather's old fisherman's knife.

He sighs, and looks up at the dusty black-and-white photo of his grandfather: young, standing tall and strong in a soldier's uniform. That was back when he served in Anatolia, where he was shot and wounded on the front lines. War hero. Then he returned here to this village for peace, only to suffer through two more wars. He re-built this little three-room house twice with his humble, honest hands, to raise his eight children. Lefteri's grandmother cooked the family meals here in this room, at this crumbling little fireplace, with only one pot that sits now in the hearth as an ornament.

"They had nothing. They were happy," Lefteri thinks.

He takes a long drag from his cigarette and butts it out into the overflowing ashtray. Crying, then angrily shaking his head, he swigs from the bottle of *tsipouro* and slams it down and presses the sharp blade to his wrist: his hand is strained backwards, his veins protrude like electrical wires. He clenches the wooden handle fiercely, as if threatening someone. There is nobody else in the room.

After a long stare-down, he hurls the knife at the wall. Weeps.

Lefteri wakes in the hot early morning on the floor. His clothes are soiled from urine and feces, and also from the bottle of *tsipouro*: he knocked it over in the middle of the night and it pooled around him.

Struggling to his feet and stumbling in a rush to the washroom, he lunges towards the toilet, banging his forehead on the porcelain rim. He throws up; most of it lands in the toilet bowl, some on the rim and on the floor. He rests his sweaty cheek on the damp, cold rim, on top of his warm vomit. A long string of saliva clings to his open mouth. Dozing off, then waking again, he loudly, painfully dry heaves: only a little blood comes out.

Lefteri rests his cheek on the rim again, trying to stop the heavy nausea. He focuses on the sound of bleating from outside. Dimitra's sheep. But something is different: it sounds like only one of them. And something is wrong. The bleating – it's jarring. Long, echoing cries. Is it hurt?

Lefteri rolls onto the damp bathroom tiles. Sleeps.

Late afternoon. Lefteri wakes, dehydrated; his neck pierces as he straightens it and stands, leaning heavily on the sink. He turns the tap on and alternates between drinking out of his cupped hands and splashing water on his face. The pain in his head is severe. He opens the medicine cabinet and takes four pills.

Removing his soiled clothes, he apprehensively handles his sticky, clumpy underwear, throwing them in the garbage. He looks in the mirror. A long look: corpulent, hairy shoulders; mottled skin; sickly dark lines around his eyes. His curly black hair, what's left of it, is dishevelled, his pale scalp screams out from underneath. His face is unshaven, which accentuates his double chin.

He can't go into town looking like this. He would rather not leave the house at all, but he needs more *tsipouro*. He showers and dresses, takes two more pills for his aching head, and walks to the kitchen and looks in the refrigerator. Just two pieces of leftover pizza and a rotting apple. He takes the pizza and sits at the round table. The only light in the room emanates from the slits in the shutters, where the afternoon sun tries to bully its way in. He eats, then lights a cigarette and listens: one sheep, still wailing. Has it been screaming like this all along?

Lefteri opens the balcony doors and the sun pours in, making him squint with pain. He dons his sunglasses and walks out and sees Dimitra's sheep below, in the large plot next to her house. All of them are huddled closely underneath the lone tree in the field, except one, which stands apart from the group in the full afternoon sun, pressed up against the chain-link fence nearest to Dimitra's house. There are patches of blood on its coat from trying to break through the fence.

Dimitra sits on her balcony with her grandchildren. Lefteri calls out to her but she doesn't hear. He calls out louder, straining, negotiating the heavy pain in his head. Dimitra hears this time.

"Lefteri, is that you?" she calls out in her high-pitched voice. "When did you get to town?"

"What's wrong with that sheep down there?"

"Oh, she's just upset because I took her lamb away. It's okay, she'll stop soon."

Lefteri looks back at the sheep and sighs.

"Say greetings to your father for me," Dimitra shouts. "Lefteri. Lefteri!"

"What?" Lefteri says, looking back at her.

"I said, greetings to your father from me."

"Yes, of course."

Lefteri makes the long walk into town under the imperious sun, over the small hill and then down the bigger one. White houses flank both sides of the narrow street leading to the main square. Old people sit silently on their balconies, watching.

He finally makes it to the town square, hot and out of breath. Sweat dampens the back wings and underarms of his shirt. He goes straight to Gianni's grill.

"Four gyros," Lefteri softly says to Gianni from behind his dark sunglasses.

"Large?" Gianni says. He always speaks loudly. Sweat drips down his unshaven cheek, over his scar.

"Yes."

"With everything? Potatoes? Ketchup?"

"Yes. And do you have any more of your father's *tsipouro*?"

Gianni points to a shelf to Lefteri's right where there are a dozen two-litre plastic bottles of what used to be soft drinks, now refilled with Gianni's father's homemade *tsipouro*.

"I'll take three of those," Lefteri says, rubbing his right temple.

Gianni nods, then turns and begins the order. Lefteri goes outside, lights a cigarette and looks out on the square. The blacks and Chinese peddle their products in the far corner. Over in the other corner, two kids laugh and chase each other around the bronze plinth that supports the bust of Lefteri's grandfather. Other kids climb up and down the bigger war memorial just behind it: giant marble crosses surrounding a larger slab with names carved into it. Their mothers holler at them from the adjacent café to get down; they don't listen.

"Lefteri, is that you?" someone says.

A startled Lefteri turns and sees Nikos, who is looking at him almost suspiciously. Lefteri's grandfather baptized Nikos.

"I hardly recognized you," Nikos says, his small hazel eyes still scanning Lefteri.

"How are you, Nikos?" Lefteri musters.

"Fine, fine. Been a while," he says, fidgeting with the *komboloi* in his hands. Every bead on the *komboloi* is a little Greek flag. "I'm down here this weekend visiting my mother. What are you doing here?"

"Just needed to get out of town for a few days."

"You're living in Athens, right?"

Lefteri nods and takes a drag of his cigarette. He looks back at Gianni on the grill: still preparing his order.

"I hear you're working for your father," Nikos says. "I guess things are busy now, with the elections."

"What are you doing these days?"

"I'm living in Patras. I was working for city council, but...but they let me go, you know how it is. Are you married?"

"No."

Lefteri looks back at Gianni: still working away.

"I'm married," continues Nikos. "I have two little ones, a boy and a girl. It's great having kids. Best thing that ever happened to me. But it's tough too, with the economy. What kind of work specifically are you doing..."

"Do you speak to my brother much?"

"Not the way we used to when we were kids. You know how it is, different cities now, obligations. I hear he has three little ones."

"No, four now."

"Wow," he says, shaking his head. "Four. And your sister?"

"She has three."

"Only three!" he says, and laughs.

Lefteri looks back at Gianni, who thankfully nods him over.

"It's nice seeing you, Nikos," Lefteri says as he butts out his cigarette.

"Why don't we sit for a coffee?"

"I can't."

Lefteri turns and goes inside. He pays Gianni and takes the heavy bags. When he walks out again, Nikos is still there.

"Hey, Lefteri," Nikos says, looking down at his worry beads and then back up. "If I don't see you again this weekend…say hello to your father for me, will you?"

Night falls. Lefteri sits in front of the fireplace, food wrappers scattered on the floor around him. He takes a drag of his cigarette and listens to the sheep, still bleating. Its cries have slowed down, and aren't as loud any more. But that only makes it sound more pitiful. More alone.

Lefteri looks up at the dusty old shrine of Mary holding Jesus, hanging from the ceiling in the corner of the room. There's a long electrical wire hanging from it. He gets up and plugs it in. A dim red light envelops the room, illuminating the picture of his grandfather.

Lefteri looks at the picture and remembers standing right in this spot, all those years ago, with his father.

"Not everyone goes to the army, Lefteri, don't be naïve," his father calmly said. He stroked his moustache as he spoke and didn't look up from the stack of papers he was reading.

"*Papou* did it," Lefteri said, pointing to the photo.

"Your grandfather fought so that you wouldn't have to," his father said, looking up now, pointing at Lefteri with the papers still in his hand.

"But…"

"The army isn't for us, Lefteri. Not anymore. Just get an education like your brother and sister."

The cigarette Lefteri holds burns into his fingers. He winces in pain and angrily throws it into the fireplace, banging his hand on the mantel and again straining in pain, this time clutching his wrist. Hunched over, he looks at the empty chair where his father sat all those years ago and goes to it and kicks it repeatedly, then pushes it over. Tears. He takes the knife in one hand, and the half-empty bottle of *tsipouro* with the other. He takes a long sip and holds the knife to his wrist. Silence. Silence. Or almost silence. The only sound is the sheep, wailing meekly.

"Just stop," Lefteri slurs out loud. "Nobody's listening. There's no point."

It continues. He cries.

"Just stop," he keeps repeating, almost in a whisper.

Suddenly he screams out and impetuously stands up, knocking the bottle over, and with knife in hand stumbles out of the room and kicks the front door open, slamming it against the wall behind. He walks in heavy steps, one hand in a fist and the other clenching the knife, down the road and around to the fields below. He yanks at the waist-high chain-link fence, trying in vain to break it but can't. He hops over, not noticing that he opens a gash on his leg as he does. The rest of the sheep are seated, asleep around the field, but the one Lefteri comes for is in the same place, pressed up against the fence. He approaches, and when he is just steps away it turns around, sees him, and tries to run. Lefteri lunges at it and straddles its back. They tumble to the ground. Lefteri drops the knife as he wrestles with the beast. He holds it from behind, his arms wrapped around its torso. It kicks, it writhes, but Lefteri manages to hold his grip.

He reaches blindly on the ground behind him for the knife. He finds it, and just as the sheep manages to squirm loose, Lefteri swings his arm around and plunges the blade into its chest. The sheep lets out a painful groan and jolts away, but Lefteri keeps the knife plunged inside while holding the animal close with his free arm. He tries to slice upwards, but the sheep jerks backwards and the knife falls loose. Lefteri reaches for it and the sheep writhes violently, seeing an opportunity for escape, but Lefteri squeezes and tightens his grip around its body with both arms, causing a bubbly-looking organ to protrude from the hole in its torso.

Lefteri reaches for the knife once more but can't get it, and once again the animal shakes violently to get loose. Lefteri looks at the bloody bubble protruding from the torso and reaches around the beast's body and takes the organ in his hand and squeezes. The bubble pops and the sheep lets out a painful yelp and writhes violently. Lefteri falls sideways, causing him to yank whatever it was he was grabbing at out of the animal, still connected to it like an umbilical cord. Lefteri squeezes the stringy, viscid organ, then plunges his hand into the hole and pulls at the animal's warm entrails. Whatever he is grabbing stretches, then severs.

The animal gurgles as Lefteri continues to damage it, badly. Finally, it lets out one final yelp, and then gurgles again before its head falls back, lithe and still.

Lefteri too falls back, releasing his grip. He is out of breath. The warm pool of blood around him grows as he lies silent and still, breathing heavily. He looks over towards the other sheep as they shift as a group towards the other end of the field, the bells around their necks emanating loudly into the night like alarms. Over his other shoulder there is stirring from Dimitra's house.

Lights go on; shadows appear in doorways.

Lefteri lies motionless, listening to the bells on one side of him and the twigs snapping on the other, as the shadows approach, closer and closer.

Greg Hollingshead

MOTHER / SON

People who do the London *Sunday Times* crossword puzzle later in the week, he tells his mother as they wait at the hospital for the doctor, do it faster and are more likely to finish it than people who do it soon after it appears. So the question is, Are the people who do it earlier more likely, over the next few days, to say or write the words that got them the right answers, and so those words are in the air and generally more available to the people who do the puzzle later? Or is it mass telepathy?

I'll only do that one if somebody saves it for me, his mother says. It's hard, though. I'd rather do the *Star*'s.

He tells her that in England when milk delivery was reintroduced after the First War, the bottles were sealed for the first time, and it was a few years before a Great Tit figured out how to open one. But soon after it did, the know-how spread through the Great Tit population, all over Europe, with no relation between distance and timing of transmission.

You're kidding, his mother says. We haven't had milk delivery in years.

It's been estimated, he tells her, that non-feral cats kill a quarter of a billion birds a year. Ever since they became domesticated, cats have been killing birds strictly for the sport and for human approval.

You don't have to tell me, his mother says. I hate it when Catkins comes in with some poor creature in his mouth and lays it at my feet and looks up at me all proud, and the only thing I can think is, I just hope it's dead.

Declawed cats get more infections, he tells her, because they use their mouths more.

But he's such a good cat, his mother says. I don't know what I'd do without him. As far as I'm concerned, he's a person, just like you or me. And she recounts how, the other day when she broke down sobbing at a Humane Society ad on TV about abused and neglected pets, Catkins pressed himself against her chest and put his paws around her neck and kissed her on the lips.

He tells her that a third of the human population of the world carries *Toxoplasma gondii*, a virus picked up from cats that have picked it up from rats, which it causes to lose their fear of cats in order to improve its chances of completing its life cycle by returning to its feline host. Humans who test positive for the virus, he adds, show significantly higher rates of depression, schizophrenia, suicide, and being in car accidents. Also, presumably, a greater susceptibility to being eaten by big cats.

His mother reminds him how Catkins always sleeps with her and asks if he remembers Catkins' toy box, next to the fireplace. Because the other morning she woke up, and Catkins had already left her bed. When she came downstairs she saw why. In one corner of his box he'd piled the toys he'd inherited from his predecessor; in the second corner, his favourites; in the third, the ones from Mrs. Carey, from down the street; and in the fourth box, his catnip ones. The rubber mouse, which he'd never liked, he'd left out of the box altogether. Catkins had got up early to sort his toys.

Women infected with *Toxoplasma gondii*, he tells his mother, are more extroverted and concerned about their appearance than women who are not. Men are more jealous, suspicious, and conservative than men who are not. You can't tell if this or that person has the virus, it only shows up in the statistics. A study of thirty-nine countries indicated that people of both sexes when infected with *Toxoplasma gondii* suffer a kind of malaise. A *Toxoplasma-gondii*-infected population is easily manipulated by guilt. You can see it in the voting patterns.

His mother says she's always voted. She started the first year she was old enough and has never missed an election. Of course, the only one who wasn't an idiot was Trudeau. The father.

He tells her about a man on a talk show he saw recently, who's working to save lions in Africa. As a child he suffered from a stutter, except when he was talking to his pets. He realized they had minds, they just couldn't talk back. He vowed that if his stutter was ever cured, he'd become an advocate for animal rights.

Catkins doesn't need to say a word, his mother says. We're soulmates.

Probably as a result of increased stress on their habitats, he tells his mother, animals around the world have begun behaving unnaturally. Storks killing chickens. Elephants raping rhinoceroses. Every year more bears and wolves stalking and attacking humans. Even stingrays are now regularly killing people; the Australian crocodile hunter's was only the first widely publicized stingray death.

I know, his mother says. The world's gone mad. Pirates, beheadings, people lighting themselves on fire. Setting off bombs in the street, killing innocent bystanders. Armies signing up children. Kids in school with automatic weapons. And the mouths on them! What's got into everybody? Why can't people be kind to each other, the way we used to be?

He tells her *kind* is from the Old English *gecynde,* meaning natural, or native. The more alienated we are from nature, he says, the unkinder we'll be, though historically you have to wonder about the Meso- and North American Indians, who were as close to nature as you could get but would swing the children of their enemies by the feet to smash their heads against trees and spend up to five days torturing their prisoners to death, forcing them to sing while eating their own intestines, and so on. The cruelty was unspeakable.

In a mock-genteel voice, his mother asks why people can't just behave nice-*leh*. None of this dog-eat-dog crap, she adds bitterly. Of course, when we were kids, everybody was poor. We were all in the same boat, and what little we got we were grateful for. We looked out for each other, and we didn't think anything of it. And she tells the story of how she used to tag along with her brothers when they scoured the railroad tracks for lumps of coal. Our parents didn't make us do it, she says, we just did it, because we were good kids. These monsters today get everything handed to them on a platter.

Chimps, gorillas, orangutans, bonobos, and humans all belong to the family *Hominidae*, he tells her. Over ninety-five percent of our genetic material we share with chimps, and chimps aren't known for their loving natures. Certainly not compared to, say, dogs.

Or cats, his mother says.

I don't know about cats.

I do.

Homo sapiens are the last of the genus *Homo*, he continues after a short pause. Thanks largely to us, all other members of our genus are extinct. Both Neanderthals and *Homo erectus*, for two, existed for hundreds of thousands years longer than we're likely to, but the only way they're alive today is in our genes, because we interbred with them. Between eight and four million years before that, the gorillas and subsequently the chimps and bonobos split off from the line that led to us. The funny thing is, we share our head lice with chimps, but our pubic lice we share with gorillas.

That's not very nice, his mother says.

The difference between us and the chimps and apes, he says, is that even when we teach them language they can take or leave their own agency. Not like us. Sometime between two hundred thousand and fifty thousand years ago, our thoughts grew loud and clear enough to react not just to the world but to themselves. This created the feeling we have a judge or critic inside us, responsible for our thoughts.

The presumption of a thinker meant an exponential increase in worry about him, which meant worry about the past and future, which meant an investment of memory and imagination in things beyond their immediate usefulness. Suddenly, after two million years of minimal technological change, we were living in larger social groups, elaborating and extending our trading networks, our skill with fire, our farming methods, our tool-making, our burial practices, our decorative arts, our religions. We were setting out on sea voyages and overland treks with destinations we could only imagine, and given our commitment to a thinker, it was always with a murderous view of those not like him (an arbitrary classification), wreaking havoc everywhere we went, causing mass extinctions of megafauna and exterminating any dangerous or edible creature we couldn't either tame or farm, sparing only those in mountain, forest, or island refuges.

The result today is seven billion brains dedicated to the survival of the thinker, his ideas, and those he considers like him. Even the intimation of a benign force in things that doesn't originate in thought, the thinker hedges round with rules and rituals that demand conformity and dissemination and so turns an intimation that he can't understand into moral and social conflict, which he can. No wonder species die-offs are now occurring at a rate a hundred to a thousand times greater than two centuries ago. No wonder we're quickly bringing the world we know to an end. Some of us decry this, most are oblivious or deny it or celebrate it as the fulfillment of God's plan, and the will to do anything about it is negligible. It's hard to imagine how the folly, ignorance, and destructiveness of *Homo sapiens* so far could be any more evident than from this.

His mother has been watching a nurse come down the corridor toward them. What's *her* problem? she says.

Two hours later, the nurse returns leading his mother, who has bandages on her eyes. She has had her cataracts removed.

As he guides his mother toward the revolving hospital door, the nurse at Reception calls out to them.

Now what is it? his mother mutters.

The nurse explains that she needs to make her an appointment for eyeglasses.

What am I supposed to do with eyeglasses? his mother demands of the nurse.

See distance? the nurse says, looking up with a tentative smile from her appointment book. You'll be able to see distance now. But you will need glasses.

Why would I want to see distance? You think at my age I'm still driving?

The idea that she would want to see distance is annoying to his mother. If something is *distant*, it has nothing to do with her. Any fool should be able to understand that.

If you think I'm wasting my time with glasses, she tells the nurse, you've got another think coming.

As they make their way across the parking lot, he tells his mother that over a kilogram of our body weight is alien bacteria.

It doesn't matter how much weight I lose any more, his mother says. I'm still going to have this belly. It's why I always get the dry cleaners to put an elastic in my sweaters.

There are more beneficial bacteria in our bodies than harmful ones, he tells her. They make us who we are. But who we are is different for different people.

Each of us is a unique ecosystem, and antibiotics are a form of clear-cutting. They don't discriminate between the good and bad bacteria in the body of a particular individual. But one day we'll design antibiotics that can do that. Doctors will stop pretending to be healers and become gardeners.

You should see my patio, his mother says. It's so pretty, now that I've got all my plants in.

By the time he delivers his mother home, the sun has gone down, but the evening is warm and bright. The cat's tail whips with joy to see her. It arches its back and drags its flank along her calves. Oh, go and lie down, you *fool* cat! she cries, clutching her son's arm. Supporting her with care, he guides her toward the patio. When they step out the French doors, he halts in astonishment before a massive blood-gold orb on a slow bounce off the roof of the house across the lane.

What's *wrong?* his mother says.

He sits her in her favourite patio chair and removes the bandages.

For a moment she is speechless, and then she says, Would you get a load of that moon. Isn't that something else.

He tells her people think the moon looks large on the horizon because the atmosphere magnifies it, but in fact the only reason it looks large on the horizon is that our brains assume it's near the ground and could be a threat, or food, or otherwise put to use, and so they swell it for a better look. It's the same with human faces, he adds. The reason they're disproportionately large in our field of vision is they're important to us.

The cat has jumped up onto his mother's lap. Aw, she says. Look at mummy's sweetheart. Catkins wants to look at the moon too. Don't you, pet?

The cat shows no interest in the moon. Still in her lap, it rolls onto its back and strikes a pose, with its paws alongside its face.

I know you're not a cat lover, his mother tells him, but don't you dare tell me this isn't the most adorable sight you've ever seen.

He admits that between the delusional agency of *Homo sapiens*, the survival skills of cats, and *Toxoplasma gondii*, it's hard to say who's in charge.

Don't be ridiculous, his mother says. It's this little demon right here. Aren't you, mummy's clever little man?

Her gnarled, practised fingers are rubbing hard at the base of the cat's ears.

It purrs in ferocious surrender.

Matthew R. Loney

A FIRE IN
THE CLEARING

Gravel ricocheted off the undercarriage as the steel-coloured Volvo sped up. The steady percussion of stones masked the noise of the camping gear shifting in the trunk as the vehicle pitched and swayed over potholes. The road getting worse meant he was nearly there. All his favorite places in the province were like that, at the distant ends of deteriorating gravel roads. He loved the kind that led to where you could drive no further, where you would slow to a crawl, become blocked by a body of white-capped water or an impassable forest of spruce, the kind that lead to the cabin.

The blue glow of the dashboard matched the head-lights' intensity. A shower of insects blazed white on the windshield. As a boy he'd seen deer along this road – a doe had once darted out with her fawn. Their coal-black marmoreal stares froze in the high beams and for the only time he could remember he'd heard his father swear out loud.

Goddamn deer. Just in time.

This far north the lakes fanned outward like amoebas. Wild eskers of forested shoreline separated each inlet and cove, wending around each other in a geographical labyrinth. The radio still crackled with reception. He'd expected that much at least, but surprisingly his cell phone still showed three bars. Progress, sure.

A kilometre more, he thought.

He would assemble the tent using a fire for light. To gather wood he would have to be cautious and use the headlights. Running out of battery this deep backwoods could land him in all sorts of trouble he'd rather not think about. He'd get the flames going by nesting birch bark with clumps of old needles and dead leaves. Later he would add kindling, a few heavier branches. Larger blow-down would be easy to find and there was never much wind that would make it past the tree line at the shore. One dead pine or cedar would be fuel enough. It was good there wasn't any wind, he thought. There was also moisture on the grass and in the soil – just a few centimetres of peat over a bedrock of limestone, only enough for a thin set of roots to grow. Dry, peat soil could spread a fire, even keeping it alive underground if given a steady supply of oxygen.

When he pulled into the clearing and stopped, the grass came as high as the driver-side window. Through the rolled-down opening he smelled the damp stalks and the wet tannin of mud. He switched off the headlights and sat in silence as the familiar shape of the cabin began to edge itself out from the blackness. He breathed in full lungs of air in the audible quiet: crickets, a frog croaking its coordinates somewhere in the dark like a two-toned ratchet, the sound of waves muted in the distance.

Slowly the posts of the weathered grey porch appeared, then the tilted eaves of the roof stopping where the blackberry bushes had wildly overgrown. Next, he saw the worn log siding, the Indian chair crafted from bent saplings and bark. The faded colour in the corner was a forgotten beach towel, crumpled and solidified beneath ten winters of snow. The cabin looked smaller than he remembered. The roof had caved at the back, maybe that was why. He was always surprised at the difference the passing of years made to the memory of objects. Rooms shrank. Ceilings drifted downward. How much smaller everything was that had been magnificent and indestructible as a kid. So fallible what had once seemed faultless. Nothing ever stayed the same as you remembered it.

He reached for the cell phone vibrating on the front seat. As he flipped it open, he stepped out and undid his fly, turning toward the forest.

—Hi – she said – Are you there?

—Yeah. Just now.

—What's it look like?

—Hasn't moved.

—So it's the same.

—Nearly. Roof's fallen in a bit.

—What's that noise?

—I'm taking a piss.

—Jesus...

—Long drive, hon.

Her receiver made a noise as it scuffed against her chin and then he heard a soft cuss word like her voice was far from the mouthpiece. He shouldered the phone and did up his fly.

—...I just stubbed my toe on the bed – she said.

—Sit down then. Stop pacing.

—So tonight? Will you?

—The morning's better. In the light.

—You promised though.

—I know...I know I did.

Closing the phone, he was alone again in the quiet. Through breaks in the cloud he caught brief glimpses of stars. The clearing looked brighter; his eyes had better adjusted. Dim bursts of light flashed through the branches as the beam from the Knife Island lighthouse whipped around from the far side of the bay. As a boy he used to lie in bed in the loft, the plaid curtain pinned back from the window, counting the flashes before falling asleep. The sound of the evening news muffled upward from the radio where a lamp glowed beside the easy chair his father reclined in. If he snuck out of bed and picked silently across the floor, he could peer over the wooden railing at the mass of his father's hair, thick as bear fur, spiking over the headrest. Cans of meat stew still yawned open on the counter from dinner. *Get to bed,* his father scolded without turning. How can you tell, Dad? *I just can.* Maybe it was a raccoon. *You're a raccoon. Now get to bed.*

From where he stood in the clearing, he could see up to the tiny window and the plaid curtain he'd tacked back on the nail. So much had happened, he thought. Some time ago. Ages ago. The same cabin, the same log walls. His own childhood seemed so remotely impossible.

After the kindling caught fire, he brought a heavier log to lay on top the pile. He assembled the tent to one side of the fire and then crawled inside to lay out the sleeping bag. From inside, the fire was a soft, constant glow through the nylon. He soaked up the pleasure of the tent, its paper-thin membrane that could trick you into believing that whatever lurked outside it couldn't get you. His own daughter Alexis had loved camping for the same reason. It was the idea of protection, she confessed, more than anything.

Webs snagged his hair as he stepped onto the sagging porch and felt above the lintel for the key. He hadn't needed to lock it since there was nothing inside worth stealing. Vandals and thieves weren't even a minor threat up here. People were just accustomed to locking up their things. It made them feel safer having the key to something – worthless or important, it didn't matter. The lock resisted in his hand. He forced the key inside and had to use all his might to twist through its rust for it to open. When it finally gave with a *thwack,* he hesitated. What if everything were the same?

He felt like a burglar when the door creaked ajar and a ripple of light from the fire outside fell onto two dinner plates still vertical in the drying rack. The kettle on the stove was a frozen grey hen. Cutlery was scattered like rusted tools on the peeling laminate. Covered with dust, a cracked bar of soap still lay in its dish. As he stepped inside, the musk of the place pulled into his nostrils: Mold, soot, wet carpet with its watersnake smell, damp paper, sulfur, some tinge of metal like the aftertaste of eating snow. Breathing it all in, his eyes closed involuntarily. Suddenly he was a boy and his father stood at the stove boiling water, his broad shoulders caped in the red lumberjack's coat that always hung behind the door. His dark terrifying beard, his thick hair pushed up at the back where the pillow had pressed. *You helping me make the coffee? Come here then. Measure carefully.* Can I have some too? *When it's ready, if you like.* The morning heat buzzed off the grasses outside, the whole clearing a hot August meadow. The sound of his father's boots on the floor, the steam from his first cup of coffee held cautiously in his hands.

As his father had been with him, he'd been as severe with Alexis. Daughters were gorgeous yet unpredictable as pastures. She'd spent the summers with him at the cabin as a girl trapping bullfrogs along the shore in crude rock paddocks while he chopped and stacked firewood. Her hair would turn bleached and matted with the sun, freckles spraying bright constellations across her nose. When the autumn arrived and the nights turned colder she'd never wanted to leave. But while in the hospital, she'd refused to even look at him. He stood beside her in the snow as the smoke from her cigarette bathed up over the bandages on her wrists, the frozen turquoise of her hospital gown, the plastic I.V. tubing that held her upright like the strings of a marionette, the fiery red of her dreadlocks. *You can't stop me, Dad. Not if you tried. I'm in charge of what happens to me. When will you get that? You haven't realized I'm not your daughter anymore.* Even his memories of her seemed to be turning colder.

The roof buckled critically over the small table his father had used as a desk. From the clearing he hadn't been able to tell, but from inside the whole back corner looked like a kicked-in cardboard box. Magazines were puffy with moisture. Rodents had shredded the newspapers. Cedar and pine needles blanketed most surfaces. *How can something endure such loneliness?* He wondered where he'd been, what tasks he'd been absorbed in elsewhere while the roof silently, gradually, caved in.

The sky through the roof beams brightened the room. From the opening a raccoon spied at him. Startled by the door, it perched guiltily out of reach. Behind him, the fire outside was centered in the doorway, a perfectly contained rectangle of light.

Still hanging on the nails that punctured the log siding, his father's hunting caps hung, limp and greasy. The old man once asked him to burn a stack of papers in the fireplace, so he'd gone and lifted the entire pile off the table. He squatted and fed them one by one into the fire: Old issues of *Canadian Geographic*, phone books, pharmacy prescription bags, grocery and hardware receipts, a few pages his father had scribbled on. He watched them curl into ashy feathers on top of the glowing logs. *Wait now…Stop. Did you take those pages too?* No. *The ones I was writing on?* Panic. No. Then the chair shoving backwards as his father stood up and the sound of his boots on the floor and the weight of his presence beside him as he stared silently for some time into the fireplace. I'll write them for you again, Dad. *No,* he paused. *A loss like that you don't make up for with something else…*

Outside, the fire popped. A rash of embers exploded into the air. The raccoon shook its coat in a huff of fur, stared back one last time and then disappeared onto the roof. Its paws made a sound on the tin that reminded him of being underwater in a river – pebbles tumbling and clacking against themselves, wearing off their edges.

His pocket vibrated again.

—It's me – she said.

—I know.

—Do you think you could do it tonight? I mean, would you?

—Just one night, hon. The tent's set up.

—Have you been inside yet?

—Yeah. The roof's a mess.

—I said it would be rotting. No one's used it in so long.

—I didn't think it'd been that long.

—So will you? – Her voice faded out and he could tell by its tone she was looking down.

—Alexis wouldn't have wanted this. She wouldn't have cared…

—No, not for her. Jesus Christ, it's for you!

—It won't change anything.

—It will!

—But how?

—You've just become so, I don't know… – silence filled the receiver – …unbearable.

He stared at the empty fireplace, the ash heaped and spread like a litter box. Grey raccoon prints faded out across the floor.

—Have I?

Why the cabin? he'd asked her one night in bed, her back towards him smooth as a dawn lake, the pink curve of her hip that after twenty years still fit perfectly into his palm. What difference would it make now? Why more loss after so much already? *Because I don't want to resent you* – she'd said – *And because you need to know what it's like to lose something for good. On purpose. Forever.* You don't think I did? We both lost her. Alexis was ours. *It's not the same,* her hip rolled from his hand. *I mean stop trying to save her and lose something completely.*

He ignored everything on the inside that told him he was right, that it wouldn't make any difference, that cabins didn't equal children. That the ocean had only done to Alexis what she'd tried to do to herself so many times yet never managed. That death would always come when you couldn't prevent it, rolling you over and over until your skull, at last, met something harder. That when she'd left for India right out of the hospital, she had turned her back on everything he'd done to try and help her. What's India got for you anyway? What's there you can't find here? *Everything, Dad. And by God I mean that. Everything.*

—Alright. If it means that to you...

—Not for me – she refuted – Jesus. This is for you.

—For me.

—How can you not get that?

A loss like that. Equal.

The path to the shore was free of blow-down. It was just a tree-lined tunnel leading to the lake crisp with moonlight. He spotted a dead cedar off the path and grabbed a hold of its trunk, tugging its grey burl of branches onto the trail. This would do it. He didn't agree he needed to lose something more. Alexis had been both of theirs. You don't make up for something broken by breaking something else, he reasoned. But this would prove it for her and that's what was needed to move on.

The tree barely fit through the door of the cabin. He bent his knees and pulled with force. A branch hooked under the drying rack and the two dinner plates smashed to the floor. Like the wake of a boat a trail of copper leaves followed him in. He could have started it on the porch but it would be a better fire this way, from the inside. A curl of birch bark held the flame alight as he brought it past the tent to the porch and then through the door. Was it true he was unbearable? That she'd resent him? Would they recover on the surface yet somewhere deep beneath, down the line, this would thunder into them again, collapsing roofs, sweeping away buildings, another child, igniting forgotten underground fires?

—Fuck you – he exhaled as he lit the tree. *Fuck you.*

The dry cedar caught fire with more speed than he expected. The branches hissed and twined as the hungry flames built. It was close enough that the easy chair soon caught and then the wooden cabinets, which brought the fire over to the wall. He'd never seen one spread so quickly. It poured over the surfaces like a liquid and then sat still to dig in its stubborn teeth. It licked at the hems of the curtains then shot up the walls toward the ceiling. It leapt the wooden stairs and then started in on the roof.

At first from outside he could barely tell it was on fire. Drizzles of smoke escaped from under the roof's overhang, more like a wet sock that steamed as it dried. Muffled pops, the faint sound of crackling, then the warm, earthen glow of someone curled up inside reading a book with a beer and old moccasins. In the loft window the flames took hold of the plaid curtain and mauled it down.

A loss like that. Sure.

He stood confronting the burning cabin in the dark of the damp grass and dialed the phone.

—Did you?

—Yeah. Just now.

—Thank God – she said – Thank you, oh thank God.

—I don't feel any better.

—You will – her voice sounded lighter, relieved – I promise you will.

He turned his back to the clearing and followed the path to the lake. The water seemed black and distant, as though it contained something sinister inside it that he would forever connect to what it had done to Alexis, as though its reflection mirrored back at him something more than just the shredded moon. The guilt of a good lie, perhaps – the kind people tell themselves with a straight face for a lifetime. Or the pale of her skin with all the sadness it had collected from some place he was never invited into. The red of her bandaged wrists and how in his mind he'd always held on to her, clinging even harder as she fought and struggled to get away. His girl. *Unbearable.*

Then, as if to wound it, he picked up a rock and threw it. The surface shattered, swallowing the hole in its splash. In endless, detached circles, the moonlight rippled outward and then gradually reformed. He could break its reflection a thousand times, with a thousand rocks, and always the moon would repair itself. Invariably the water's surface would heal. On the far edge of the lake, the beam from the lighthouse spun in slow rhythmic flashes. Down here he couldn't hear the fire, just the soft vacuum of forest and the constant rustle of waves onto shore stone.

Rob Peters

SAM'S HOUSE

Everyone at school keeps asking me how I chipped my tooth. They always want me to whistle through the little hole. I usually do it but I just whistle normally and say it's coming through the hole when really it isn't. I'm a good whistler. They're pretty stupid to think someone could whistle that loud through their teeth.

I chipped it Friday after school. I had to clean the chalk erasers until 3:15 because I threw an apple at Jason W. and he told Mrs. Wilkinson. After I finished smashing all the erasers together, my friends had gone home already. There was no one to play with except Tommy, but he was already having a sleepover with Jason W. so I just walked home by myself. I kept sneezing from the chalk.

Only my brothers were home because they're in high school and they get last period off on Fridays. I don't know why. My dad doesn't get home until seven because he works in Vancouver. My mom doesn't live with us anymore.

My brothers and one of their friends were playing Dungeons and Dragons in the rec room. "Can I play?" I asked.

My oldest brother Scott said no.

"Why not?"

My other brother Barry said he needed to show me something and told me to come look at the D&D book he was holding. "This just came out," he said. "They changed the minimum age you have to be." He told me to look closer on the cover so I brought my face in to where he was pointing. Then he pulled the book away and held up his middle finger in my face. Their friend laughed. Barry kept holding his finger up so I got mad and bit it and then ran upstairs. He didn't even chase me. My brothers hardly ever let me play with them. They say eleven is too young for D&D but I know that's not really why.

I put two bags of chips in the stomach of my windbreaker and got my BMX out from the garage. I live on Uplands Drive, and every day after school my friend Sam delivers papers on my street. I know because I help him with his route a lot. Sam's nice. He has a Nintendo. He's small and doesn't talk a lot though. I helped him beat the first world in Zelda but we haven't beat the second world yet. I heard there's an invisible wall in the fifth dungeon that we can't find.

Sometimes Sam doesn't come for a while so I hide in a big tree on the corner until I can see him coming.

The tree is hollow inside like a fort, and there are lots of those little seeds that fly like helicopters when you throw them. He didn't come for a long time so I just sat on the dirt and watched through the branches. It was a white day, not sunny or rainy but just white. I pretended cars were tanks that would shoot me if they saw me.

When Sam finally came up the street, his paper basket was full and he couldn't ride his bike straight. The papers are heavy on Fridays so it was good that I was there to help.

I rode my bike out back of the bush so it would look like I was just there by accident. I asked Sam if he wanted some chips.

"Hi, Corry. Sure."

"I'll help you," I said.

"Okay."

We ate our chips and then started the papers. I know Sam's route by heart. I'm faster than he is because he always stops and picks up the *TV Times* when it falls out. I just leave it. I don't even care if the whole paper comes apart after I throw it. Sam only has thirty houses to do because it's the *Sun* and not the *Leader*. You have to do a lot more if you deliver the *Leader*, like a hundred and fifty, but you only have to do it twice a week instead of every day.

After we finished, we started riding to Sam's house. You have to go by the Grove Hill tennis courts to get there, on a dirt path beside a little forest. That's where we saw Stevie Delachey riding toward us.

"Hey. Corry sucks," Stevie yelled. He was about half a soccer field away.

"Stevie's a dickwad," I yelled back.

Stevie rode toward us and then stopped. He turned his bike sideways so we couldn't get past. We still had room to turn around but I didn't want to look like a wuss. Sam's face was red and he looked scared already. I think it's because he only has a sister.

The three of us just sat there for a second. Then I saw Stevie flick a metal lighter. He pulled out a thunder bomb from his pocket, lit it, and threw it by our feet. It made my ears ring but I didn't move. Sam turned his front wheel sideways and then kind of fell on his bike. He stood up as fast as he could.

Stevie had a smile on his face that was laughing at us. "Who's this?" he asked me.

"That's Sam."

Stevie looked at Sam until their eyes met and Sam had to look away.

"Hi," Sam said.

Stevie laughed a little bit. "Hi there, Sam."

Nobody said anything for a while. Stevie was wearing jeans with rips in the knees and white high-tops with big puffy tongues. It was cold but all he had on top was a t-shirt and a backpack. Stevie goes to the stupid school even though he's not stupid. I don't know why. He gets in fights and has a moustache already, so maybe that's why. My brother said it's because his mom lets him drink beer. I think he was lying though.

"I went to Lummi last weekend," Stevie said to me.

"Cool," I said.

Lummi is where they sell firecrackers. It's a reserve.

Stevie looked at Sam. "Yeah. Want to buy some?"

"No, thank you," Sam said, like he was talking to a teacher.

Stevie laughed a little bit again. "You sure?" He reached into his pocket and pulled out a mighty mite. He lit it and held it in his hand for a long time before throwing it up in the air. It made a bang and then a little poof of smoke against the trees behind him.

Stevie kicked the basket on the front of Sam's BMX. "You have a paper route, don't you? Twenty bucks for half a brick."

Sam looked at me like he wanted me to tell him what to do. Twenty bucks was way too much but I didn't say anything right away.

Sam felt his front jean pockets. "I don't have that much."

"Just give me what you have and I'll get the rest later," Stevie said. "I've got them in my backpack." He turned around and unzipped his bag.

I thought about what to do. When my brothers fight, my dad waits a long time before he stops them. He says you have to let people fight their own battles.

Sam's different though. He doesn't even know when there's a battle happening in the first place. That's why I have to look out for him. Sam's mom knows that I protect him. It's like a secret between us that Sam doesn't know about.

Sam pulled out a five-dollar bill from the front pocket of his jeans. He looked at me again. I told Stevie to show us the firecrackers. Then I pretended to tie my shoe and jammed a stick in Stevie's spokes when he wasn't looking.

I stood up again. "My brother Barry went to Lummi too," I said. "I can get it for cost." My brother didn't really go there, but sometimes he does.

Stevie looked mad. He zipped up his backpack. "Why are you dickheads wasting my time then?"

"You're wasting ours," I said. I hit Sam in the arm for us to go. We pedalled around Stevie's bike and down the path between the tennis courts and the forest. I turned and saw Stevie get stuck as he tried to ride away. I told Sam to look too but he didn't think it was as funny as I did.

We put our bikes in Sam's backyard and walked in the side door. Sam's family never locks the door but you have to take off your shoes when you go there. I think it's because they don't have a dog. It always smells like whatever they're having for dinner that day, so it smelled like lasagna. I like being at Sam's house because it feels like there are rules to things. Not bad rules like at school but just rules.

Sam's mom came downstairs. She was wearing a red apron over a fancy outfit that she wears for teaching piano. "It's Corry!" She touched Sam's hair and then gave me a little hug. My head was close to her neck for a second and I smelled her perfume. It was like laundry and candy and flowers.

"Hi," I said.

Sam ignored her and went upstairs.

Sam's mom frowned and asked if everything was okay.

"Yeah."

"Are you sure?"

"Yeah. We ran into a grade eighter on the way here."

"Who was it?"

"Stevie Delachey."

"Who?"

"Just some kid who goes to the special school. I took care of it though."

Sam's mom smiled and then messed up my hair. "That's my guy."

Sam and I played Zelda after that. I let Sam play most of the time because I just like watching. I'm better at remembering the maps than he is so I tell him where to go. His mom brought us cheese and crackers before going downstairs to teach piano.

Just before five o'clock, Sam's sister Margie came and told us to leave. That's when she's allowed to watch *The Young and the Restless.* I could tell she was in a bad mood because she didn't make fun of us. She doesn't like me very much because one time me and Sam caught her lip syncing "Never Surrender" to the end of a vacuum cleaner and I turned it on.

"We still have five minutes," Sam said. We were really close to finding the boss of dungeon five.

"I don't care. Get out," she said.

"We've never made it this far. This is really, really, important," Sam said.

"Yeah," I said.

Margie used the remote to turn it off.

"I'm telling," Sam said.

"Go ahead." Margie sat down and took up the whole of the couch. She had a plate of celery with peanut butter and was wearing sweat pants and a pajama top.

"Come on," Sam yelled. "Turn it back."

Margie scrunched up her face. "Turn it back," she repeated.

"You're a cow," Sam said.

Margie got mad and stood up, so we ran away. She didn't follow us though. We went downstairs. There was a girl sitting on a bench by the front door. She was waiting for a piano lesson from Sam's mom. We could hear scales coming through the closed door.

"Hello," Sam said to the girl. I think his mom tells him to say that.

"Hi."

"Let's go outside," Sam said to me.

We sat on the ground and put on our shoes. No one said anything. There was just the sound of piano exercises.

"Let's make a jump," I said to Sam when we were outside. I wanted to stay at his house as long as I could. If I stayed until after his mom's last piano lesson, she'd invite me to stay for dinner.

We dragged some wood from the backyard. Then we rolled some of the rocks that are supposed to keep cars from going onto Sam's front lawn onto the street. We added pieces of plywood on one side. It was starting to get dark but there was still enough light to see.

I went first. I'm good at getting air because I know how to bunny hop at the right time. I pretended Sam's mom was watching because it makes me ride faster when I do that. Sam took a few turns too, but he's not very good. He just rides over it like it's the end of a curb.

After a few minutes we heard firecrackers down the street. Not just one or two but entire packs all at once. Then we heard those bottle rockets that screech in the air three times and blow up at the end. I saw who was doing it. It was Stevie.

He didn't see us yet, but we couldn't just run away and leave our jump in the middle of the street. I didn't tell Sam that Stevie was there. I should have told him because Stevie lit a thunder bomb behind us when we weren't looking and threw it at Sam's feet. He was so scared that he fell sideways off his bike again.

"Hey," Stevie said.

"Why the hell did you do that?" I said.

"I found a stick in my tire." Stevie nodded towards Sam. "I think it was him."

Sam turned red and looked down at his feet. There were little scraps of paper from the thunder bomb blowing all over the road.

Stevie knew I did it but he just wanted to bug Sam. Sam knew I did it too but he didn't want to rat on me. The three of us didn't say anything for a second. Then Stevie pulled out a bottle rocket from his backpack and lit it. He waited until the wick sparked into the rocket part and threw it at the last second. It bounced off a tree and exploded near the roof of Sam's house. I saw the little pink stick roll into the gutter.

"I don't think you should do things like that," Stevie said to Sam.

Sam looked at me to say something.

I started to tell them it was me, but then Stevie interrupted. "I'll make you a deal," he said. "You buy twenty bucks worth of something and we're even." Stevie took off his backpack and unzipped it.

I saw Sam's mom watching us through the window. She was in the piano room with the girl we saw earlier. They probably heard the firecrackers. I smiled to make her feel better because she looked a little bit worried.

"No, thank you. I don't want any," Sam said.

"I told you. We can get them for way cheaper from my brother," I said.

Stevie looked like he didn't know what to do for a second. He let go of his bike and let it crash onto the road. Then he walked to the jump and moved the rocks so the board was steeper. He walked back to his bike. "Fine," he said, as he passed us. He rode his bike the other way to get a big start and then pedalled as fast as he could. He hit the jump and flew – like forever. It was the most air I've ever seen. Afterward, he rode straight toward us and then skidded sideways at the last second.

Stevie had a look on his face like he was really cool or something. "Let's see you go then," he said to Sam.

I looked toward the house. They were still watching from the piano room window. I smiled again to make Sam's mom feel better but she didn't smile back. I looked at Sam. His face was red.

"It's my turn," I said.

I rode the other way, even further than Stevie did, and then stopped. I pointed my bike towards the jump. The sky was splotchy and dark blue and there wasn't a lot of light anymore. Sam and Stevie were far away and looked like black cut-outs. I pedalled towards the jump as fast as I could, which is fast.

I remember the streetlight. It flashed twice as if it was going to come on but then it didn't and went off. Stevie and Sam were lit up for a second and I could see them standing by their bikes. Then a bottle rocket flew by my feet and exploded behind my back tire.

I could hear Stevie laughing and that made me mad. I couldn't really even see the jump and went off the side of it. My face hit the handlebar and my front tooth went through my lip onto the metal. I remember being on the ground and feeling my chin, and it was warm and wet. And Stevie was standing over me and still laughing.

The next thing that happened was Sam's mom came with a big yellow towel. Stevie and Sam and the girl were all standing around her. Sam's mom sat beside me with my head in her lap and she soaked up the blood on my face. It didn't hurt that much yet. It just felt like my face was hard. Stevie still wore a big jerky smile. I think there's something wrong with him because he doesn't get scared when bad things happen.

I was surprised by what happened next.

Sam turned toward Stevie. "Get the hell away from us," he said. "Go home."

Stevie kept smiling but he actually did what Sam said. He got on his bike and went down the street, lit off some bottle rockets, and then rode away. Sam turned bright red after he said it. His mom wasn't mad because I saw her trying not to laugh. I don't know why. I thought it was pretty cool for him to say that.

Sam's mom took me to the doctor to get stitches. I didn't cry. Afterward, my dad wasn't home yet so I got to stay over at Sam's place for dinner. I was glad about that.

His mom told the story to Sam's dad while everyone ate lasagna. She said I was tough and a real hero, and she didn't tell on Sam for swearing. And Margie had to cut up my dinner in little pieces because her mom told her to. She didn't even seem mad about it. It was a really nice time.

Liz Windhorst Harmer

TEACHING
STRATEGIES

In a classroom on the second floor, Mr. Devries is setting a small fire. It is nothing to be alarmed about. He sets up a large tin box – used to be a toolbox, he found it in the basement – in the middle of the classroom. He uses scraps of paper as tinder. Tin, he thinks. Tinder. Tiny tin full of tinder. He likes puns and wordplay and has a flair for the dramatic. These are not just things he thinks about himself but things that other people have told him. Sometimes he wishes he had made a list, an actual list on lined paper in a notebook somewhere where he had written down anything anyone had ever said about him.

He flicks the lighter with his thumb. Faintest scent of butane, little tongue of blue flame. He lights a piece of paper and drops it into the bottom of the box. The fire chews and then swallows it up. Like a dog with a bone, he thinks. It was one of the things someone had told him about himself long ago when he was in graduate school for theology: you're like a dog with a bone.

Crouched beside it, Mr. Devries stares down into the tin box. Not so much a pile of ashes but a scattering of them, and when he gets up to go to his desk to finish his sandwich they fly up like a tiny swarm of insects. The wisp of smoke has already disappeared into the room.

This is going to be good, Mr. Devries thinks. Students did well with metaphor, with analogy, with a physical representation of the spiritual movement. He himself found it illuminating as well. He unwraps the sandwich Mrs. Devries has made him, now a bit sodden and heavy because of the mayonnaise, and a bit of the lettuce gets stuck to the roof of his mouth. It slides against the skin there the way his skin does if burned by a hot beverage, and he tries to work it down with his tongue. He thinks about how hungry the fire was, like a dog with a bone, unsatisfied until it had totally consumed the paper. Had transformed the paper into ashes and smoke. Tears come into his eyes because that is how the Lord is, and he would tell his students this: our God is relentless in his pursuit of us.

Downstairs, Ms. Voordenhout is trying to erase her own scribblings with a long eraser so sooty with chalk it merely moves the white dust of it around on the board. The chalkboard is a palimpsest, but there is not much in grade nine math to interest or decipher. The little glyphs, one superimposed over another, make something like an artwork. She feels what she feels when she sees fossils at a museum, the sketchiness of bones preserved like flowers flattened in the pages of a Bible. She wishes she could find a way to preserve them for herself, to hang them on her wall, merely to admire them. To rejoice in them.

The students do not find the Pythagorean theorem something to rejoice about. They are not amazed by the proportions of things or the history of those people who discovered them. She showed them a DVD about the Parthenon, and their boredom was almost as palpable as the chalk dust now in her mouth. There is always quiet snickering. They do not stand in awe. Perhaps some of them would tell their parents and the parents would complain that she had made an idol out of mathematics. No one had ever done this but she is fearful about it and maybe this means that she has done so. She has already rehearsed her response to this: "Mathematics in its harmony and wonder points us to God."

She has tried to tell Richard about the students. They are so young, and you look at their unlined faces and their wide-open eyes and see that they know nothing. Most of them are like that and then, once in a while, you have a student who sees through you and makes you stumble, whose eyes are like one of those paintings that seem to be watching you no matter where you are in the room. Cassidy McNaughton is one such girl, and a week ago Ms. Voordenhout accused Cassidy of cheating on a math quiz. It was her own fault. She had them take up their own work and Cassidy, who always has that mean, accusatory expression on her face, reported that she got 100%. Everyone else slipped up on question eight. Ms. Voordenhout took her aside after class and calmly asked Cassidy if she'd cooked the books, so to speak.

She hasn't told Richard about Cassidy, though, and about what happened next, how the girl heaved her textbook at Ms. Voordenhout, nearly hitting her in the stomach. And then flipped her the bird. "I earned that grade! I earned it!" Cassidy kept saying, and though Ms. Voordenhout was now even more convinced that she'd cheated, she had no way of proving it.

"I'll be keeping an eye on you," she said. It was not the appropriate response to such a violent gesture. It is now three days later and too late to fill out an incident report, or to tell Mr. Hiemstra, the principal, or even to address the angry girl. Cassidy is still very angry, that much is clear, and sometimes she flashes her middle finger at Ms. Voordenhout when her back is turned. Today, during group work, she said, "It is so exasperating when adults think they're smarter than you. It is so frustrating to be accused of something you didn't do."

How is one supposed to *teach* such a person?

"Some of the students are so angry," she told Richard. They were out eating cheap Vietnamese soup because Richard thinks that it's inappropriate for them to eat in at either of their apartments. To be unsupervised and alone. They have been dating for over a year, and there isn't any chemistry, not any physical chemistry that she feels, anyway, and she has no one to talk to about how alone this makes her feel. That he doesn't have to try to resist pushing his body against her, spreading her legs, holding her thigh too tightly with lustful hands. He is five years older than her and there is grey in his beard, and a noodle hanging out from his lips for a moment before he sucks it noisily in.

"Teenagers can be like that."

She supposes that her lack of any confidante was the point. People are made for a relationship, the way Eve was made for Adam, and so she ought to at least try to find a mate. Though for the most part the school community, pedestrian as it may seem to outsiders – the school play, the Christmas concert, the staff meetings, the lunchtime discussions about scripture with people like Mr. Devries – is enough community to satisfy her need for the society of others.

Grade nine math was over for the day. It is Friday, and she wouldn't need to think about Cassidy McNaughton again for several days. Though she will, she won't be able to help it, the girl's sour face will rise up in her dreams and worse, it will squeeze through into the gaps between sleep and waking, condemning her with that fuck-you finger, knowing exactly what sort of person she is.

In the cafeteria, tables are as long as ships floating in an expanse of sea. Students are everywhere. Beyond the shouts and squeals there is the scraping of chairs, the clatter of trays covered in bunched napkins. and food-dirtied plates being carried to high metal wheeled shelves which will be pushed to the back room, where unseen bodies toiling in the steam and suds will rinse and scrub and disinfect them. The acoustics are amazing, sounds amplified and bouncing, rendering almost anything impossible to hear. Cassidy sits silently chewing a piece of pizza – a bit rubbery, not terrible, though she'd picked the pepperoni slices off – and watches her friends talking, watches their lips move, gives up trying to hear. Sometimes the choir practices in here precisely *because* of the acoustics. The architects had screwed that up. Adults are as likely as anybody to screw up. High school is an offensive idea. Actually schooling in general, all schooling, is offensive. Cassidy reserves for herself the right and the freedom to be offended.

It is the doctrine of original sin; it is the Reformed doctrine. That none of them, not even the adults, would ever be better than failures and sinners. People are like the Israelites, who forget Moses almost as soon as he went up the mountain and then melt down for themselves a Golden Calf so that they'll have something to worship. People make the worst decisions and then make them over and over.

Practically everyone is Dutch. Even these three friends, her best friends, all of whom are beginning to get up to go out for a cigarette, all of whom wear black makeup and dye streaks of magenta and blue into their hair to undercut the navy-and-white uniform they have to wear, all of them are Dutch. In the school of five hundred students, there are about a dozen Korean kids in the ESL program, a single black boy named Damian, the adopted son of Dutch parents, and maybe fifty non-Dutch white kids like herself. She wishes they were more diverse – she is offended by their homogeny – but at the same time she is concerned that this concern itself is racist.

She follows her friends outside and down past the soccer fields to a marshy area – a ditch, really – where they are hidden from sight. This week it's Charlene's turn to provide the smokes, and she passes one around for each of them and lights them in turn with her Bic lighter. Then Anne-Marie pulls a flattened joint out of her pocket and, with raised eyebrows, lights this as well and offers it around. She hasn't yet exhaled but holds the smoke in for longer than it seems possible to do. "You've got those Lance Armstrong lungs," Lacey says. She is always bringing up a trip she took to a museum in grade seven, where she'd seen a bunch of plasticized cadavers and had learned that Lance Armstrong, among other professional athletes, had larger than normal lungs. Cassidy does not want to smoke any, hates to be high, but takes a few tokes anyway in a gesture of camaraderie. For a moment this swell of fellow-feeling seems very important and then it wisps away. All but Anne-Marie cough and sputter; all laugh; and they stay out there until they hear the bell.

Ms. Voordenhout got to the staff room late, ate her lunch alone, and now is headed up to Mr. Devries's class to join in their devotional. It is her prep period, and she felt lit up from within when he asked her to come, like a lamp of her grandmother's that would turn on when you touched a finger to its base. That lamp had seemed magical to her, as had thermoses, as had, later, the Pythagorean theorem, as do fossils, and computers, and the idea of code. DNA code, computer code, mathematics: she stood in awe.

And now she is standing on the outside edge of Mr. Devries's classroom as the students file in. She nods at the ones she knows, smiles, and then Cassidy breezes by, smelling like a skunk. She seems to be trying to tuck her face into her collar, and Ms. Voordenhout looks at her, thinking, I've got my eye on you. Cassidy sits down, dropping her textbook and Bible and binder on her desk with a slam and then sinking down in her seat. She stares at her math teacher, who looks so awkward over there by the wall, who seems not to know anything, not even how to stand normally, and who is wearing a long beige skirt like she thinks she's frigging Amish. She looks sad, too, like she hasn't been loved enough.

After eating his sandwich and then an apple, Mr. Devries sat thinking about the girl in graduate school who'd said he was like a dog with a bone. They'd been arguing about something – he was passionate about many things, many small details in the scripture – and he'd gone home thinking it was a compliment. It meant, he thought, that he was willing to go farther in his pursuit of the truth than most people. He was willing to chew that bone until the meat was off. But now he thinks maybe she'd been angry with him. How can you know when the memory was twenty years old? And you can't remember anything about the girl except, possibly, an Afro? A red scarf? And that she'd been frustrated with him. Now, the students filing in, he is sure of it: she'd been angry and he'd been wrong. He'd been like a dog thrashing about with a bone in his mouth, unable to let a thing go.

It is not a good feeling to start the class in. He tries to pray it away. He smiles at Ms. Voordenhout and then forces himself to the middle of the classroom – the desks are arranged in a semi-circle to promote discussion – and he asks the students about fire in the Bible.

"The flames that came down on the disciples' heads at Pentecost," says one young man.

"Good. The Holy Spirit. What else?"

"The burning bush?" Cassidy says, blurting it out as though she hadn't meant to and then returning to staring at Ms. Voordenhout. She can't stop staring and now Ms. Voordenhout is blushing. She can feel Cassidy's eyes – at first she thinks it's anger but now she knows it's pity, which is much worse – and she begins to burn. Figuratively speaking, her face is as hot as the fire in the tin toolbox Mr. Devries is starting in the middle of his classroom. She feels foolish in the long skirt she'd worn because she knew it would please pious Richard who is going to pick her up at 3:15. She looks at the clock. How can she get through the next two hours? How can she bear to be herself for two more hours, the object of pity and scorn?

Ten years ago, when she started teaching here, she used to tell the students about her past life. The inner-city mission in Toronto, the inner-city mission in Chicago, moving around, going to other countries, to El Salvador, to Uganda. The different way air felt in different parts of the world. The different kind of grime that washed off her body after a hard day; red like clay or sandy or sweaty or sooty. You can feel the pollution on you in the city, but it is harder to breathe in South

America. She knew by telling her students those things she was trying to make excuses for why she isn't married.

Mr. Devries lights a piece of paper on fire and quietly puts it into the tin box. "Fire destroys. And fire refines. The Lord will set you aflame and burn away the sin and leave you refined like gold. Purified. I invite you to write down your sin on the index card in front of you and come to the front here and drop it into the fire. Put it in the fire. Put an end to your sin." He takes an index card out of his back pocket and demonstrates. "Write down a sin and watch what God does with it." The fire is small, flames only one or two inches high. Mr. Devries has done this before. Has done this many times before. He has faith; he has passion. The index cards are heavy and will not float up and start fires elsewhere in the room. A window is cracked so that the room will not fill with smoke.

No one moves for a minute; they are thinking about which sin to write down. They are wondering about the sins of their immediate neighbours. They are wondering if their neighbours are going to see the sin they write. Cassidy turns her glare on Mr. Devries, who is always up to antics like this – dramatizing the scripture – but teaches them almost nothing about the Old Testament, which is the topic of the course. She uncaps a black marker and writes, *I am tainted by the sins of Eve.* She is the first to go forward. One after another her classmates follow, some of them who have written down genuine sins – *I used the Lord's name in vain. I sometimes cut myself* – though none of them have the guts to write down the things that really shame them. Masturbating. Pornography. Drugs. Hate. Jealousy. Rage. Vanity. A girl named Rose is so moved when she watches the fire that she sobs quietly into her hands. Most of them look sombre, some horrified, and Cassidy looks sardonic.

Cassidy will not stop staring at Ms. Voordenhout, and hot rage is filling Ms. Voordenhout like lava. You want to pity me? Hot lava filling her like it will drip from her eyes, her ears. She has never been so angry in her entire life. Never in her entire life! She knows now why Jesus said that a person who is angry with his brother has murdered him in his heart, because she is imagining putting her hands around Cassidy's neck, choking her until she pleads for her life. She can feel in the heat of the anger, spreading through her and making her huge, that she may do something now that she cannot undo. She may swear. She may scream. She may flip Cassidy the fuck-you finger.

Shaking, she picks up an index card from the desk nearest her and writes down, in a huge, shaky, uncontrolled scrawl: *I despise Cassidy McNaughton.* It feels good. She looks straight at the girl and dares her to feel pity. You don't know me, the look says, and it says it hard, and it will not stop looking at Cassidy. She walks towards the tin box that way, half-staring at Cassidy, and drops the card with what feels like gravitas. It feels good to be so dramatic, to have such flair. She looks gratefully at Mr. Devries, who she loves! She loves him! She loves him so much for doing something so crazy and bold as starting a fire in a classroom.

"Oh my God," Cassidy stands up and shouts. "Oh my God, Ms. Voordenhout!"

"Cassidy," Mr. Devries says, his first thought being to correct her for using the Lord's name that way. But she's pointing at Ms. Voordenhout and then he sees – the skirt has caught on fire.

There is a warmth around her ankles: she looks down and begins to laugh. Of course! The skirt is on fire. The skirt she is wearing. For now the flames are slow and methodical, moving up along around her hemline like a line of grassfire. The breeze from the open windows only encourages things, and when she moves the flames grow. Is it possible that they will burn her? Yes. Soon it will be out of control. Everyone is watching her stand there with her hands on her cheeks. "Help me," she says. But no one knows what to do. They are babies; they are puppies. Even Cassidy, for all her scorn. Mr. Devries feels his heart sink through. It is idiotic to start a fire in a tin box in a classroom. If anybody tells Principal Heimstra, he'll be up a creek. He feels, now, what Simon Peter must have felt when he was standing on the water – as soon as you lose faith you fall right through.

It's too hot for thinking. It's too late. There is only one thing to do. Ms. Voordenhout unzips her skirt and drops it, steps out of it, her body shaking, and then stomps on the fire with all of her weight. No one thinks to look away. Rose is still quietly sobbing, and feels that there is a message in all of this, and it frightens her. The skirt-fire is out, the tin-box fire is just smoldering, and the wisps of smoke are not enough to shield Ms. Voordenhout. Later, she will think the whole thing through. It will be several long minutes before Mr. Devries thinks to give her his jacket to wrap around her waist, and for now she stands there in her white underpants, holding her hands over her crotch like a prudish etching of Eve. Later she will wonder if the students have taken pictures with their phones, and she will wonder about the jiggle of her cellulite, and the creeping vines of pubic hair not quite contained by her panties, and the unshaved portions of her thighs. She will see Richard and swell with gratitude that he has never seen her naked. She will wonder if she can ever go back. She will search the Internet looking for mission trips to India, to China, to Papua New Guinea. For now, she is still shaking from the adrenaline. She has narrowly avoided disaster.

"Oh, Ms. Voordenhout," Mr. Devries says. It is the worst thing he could say. Cassidy's eyes are on her. She lifts up her shaking hand and closes it into a fist and, all of the feelings thudding all through her body, through her face, she starts laughing again. Even now, she cannot let that middle finger fly.

Austin Clarke

THEY NEVER
TOLD ME

I am getting old. And I hate it. I use swear words to
stem the silent flow of years that overtake my actions,
and even the flow of my speech. My first recognition of
this malady of old age is the stumbling, and the climbing of stairs. And after many trials, the stammering to
find the word that does not come easily into my mind,
and that remains on the tip of my tongue. And they
never told me how to be cool and decent about this
slowing down of speech; the lengthening struggles to
find the correct word, remembering it until I match the
thought to the written word itself… the fading of faces,
the disappearance of names from the faces that my eyes
move over, like an usher's flashlight in a crowded cinema; and from the pages of names in my pocket diary. I
am old. But I hide it. I hide my fear of old age; and my
shame of it. I do not want to get old; do not want to be
recognized; to be greeted by old friends, precisely
because they are old; or, to be pointed out by a smiling
young woman, with her eyes, and a nod, and a smile,

that illustrates her question, and her concern, "Would you like my seat, sir?"

But I take the offer and take her seat; and my indignation swells, and smells like stale perspiration. I take the seat. I am very close to this young woman as she stands up. I can see the thin outline of her panties through the summer-thin dress. I become ashamed of myself. Of my desire. And I want to scream my indignation out, to everyone on this crowded bus, "Do I look so old to you?"

But shame and reality keep my lips shut.

And when I return to my house, two hours after my encounter with the kind young woman, I confront myself in the small unframed, rectangular glass over the white washbasin. The washbasin is made of smooth white enamel. The small bathroom is painted white. The paint shines. There are large brown bottles and a damp washcloth in the sink; and bottles of pills for headache, and pills for earache; and pills to pacify the cough that rumbles in my chest; and pills for head colds. And pills for losing weight; large pills, colourful pills, pills that I have left untouched, left in a bulbous green bottle. And then a round tin, flat like a puck slapped around in a hockey game. Kiwi Black Shoe Polish! And around the tin are the words, "noir, kiwi, black, kiwi, noir, kiwi, black, kiwi." I had not known that "kiwi" was another name for "black." I turn the catch, the little metal wings on the tin. "Water resistant.

Leather nourishing." And round the diameter of the tin, is the reassurance: "By appointment to H.R.H. the Duke of Edinburgh. Makers of shoe polish." The picture of a kiwi bird is drawn in yellow.

As I twist the catch, the full power of the shoe polish strikes my nostrils; and I dig my middle finger deep into the thick, silky blackness, moving my three fingers covered in the black soil of thick shoe polish over my face – I think of Negro minstrels, and of white men who wanted to turn themselves into black men. The hand that holds the black shoe polish is black. And nervous. And shaking in the horror of the act I am committing; turning myself into a blackface black man; while all I wanted to do was to slick my hair with black shoe polish, to make myself look sleek and younger; to make young women stop getting up to offer me their seat. I want to look young. I rub the black shoe polish into my skin. I look at my reflection. And I see the laughing face of a man. The face of Al Jolson. The face of a white man who sang like a cantor who is Negro, whose hand is black, and I imagine myself singing a song written by a white man, by Stephen Foster pretending to be a down home country boy black man.

> *Way down upon de Swanee Ribber,*
> *Far far away,*
> *Dere's whu my heart is turning ebber,*
> *Dere's whu de old folks stay…*

I am an old man still, and I am mouthing the words of this song; and my back takes on the shape of an old man moving to the slow beat of the song. My back is bent. The song overcomes me. My lips are large; and red. My eyes droop. My hands shake. I am Al Jolson. I am singing the minstrel blues,

> *Way down upon de Swanee Ribber,*
> *Far far away,*

and my face is by appointment to H.R.H. the Duke, and I feel comfortable with my new darkness, and I move my body slow. And I dance, and I laugh and my teeth become pearly white, and my eyeballs lose their pupils; and are now completely white. And I am rocking from one side to another side. And my voice has become deep, and I roar with laughter at my antics.

I sometimes come to my home and climb the forty-seven steps to this bathroom, and after I close the door behind me, I find I'm lost in my head, I've forgotten completely why I climbed those steps. So I retrace my forty-seven steps, counting out loud their number. The count becomes everything, mindful that one false step will send me hurtling down to smash myself against zero, the bronze panel in the front door; and then, I will have to rouse myself and re-climb and recount the forty-seven steps, and enter the bathroom a second time… and then try to remember why I had entered it the first time. But now it comes back to me. I had wanted to get a tissue of white Kleenex to polish my reading glasses with so I could see *whu my heart is turning ebber*…

In the bathroom, I look at my blackened hair, not so black as I had wanted it to be, and I turn the tin of shoe polish over, and I see it is a tin of Canadian shoe polish made at the Kiwi Polish Company (Canada) Limited, in Hamilton, just a few miles west of Toronto; and this closeness, like family, makes the black paint on my face more acceptable. I like being blackfaced. In safety and security beneath the "black, kiwi, noir" of my new complexion, behind the mask that is painted black on my face. I can now wallow in the peace of being lost in a place where I will take a seat beside a young woman, where I will inhale her alluring perfume; and when the bus stops, enjoy the touch of her arm, and wonder if at my age – which nobody knows for certain – if her sweet, soft arm, and the whiff of her auburn hair against the blackened, curled hairs on my unshaven chin, could ever reawaken that dormant, once sweet sensuality which…"dream on, old man!…" might come alive, stand as erect as the first bursts of spring flowers, with me now travelling in peace; buried deep in the deeper tranquility of forgetfulness.

Riding up and down on a bus, the Rosedale route down to the waterfront on Sherbourne Street. I even stop and get off at the large LCBO liquor store. And buy a mickey of rum, fifteen-year-old El Dorado Rum, made in Demerara. And back on the bus, I sneak a sip from the shaking bottle, caused by the hard driving over a broken pot-holed road, and caused by the strength of the rum. I hold the bottle under my winter coat. Nobody sees me. Nobody looks at me. Nobody cares. I am an old black man with my face painted black at the back of the bus.

And the bus turns around, going north from the waterfront along this same Sherbourne Street where it touches Queen Street East; past the multitudes of bums and beggars; and the homeless; and drunks; and no one knows me. I have become one of them. No one has to be kind to me, to offer me a seat. I can hum. I can sing, under my breath, like Al Jolson, the whole entire song…

> *Way down upon de Swanee Ribber,*
> *Far far away,*
> *Dere's whu my heart is turning ebber,*
> *Dere's whu de old folks stay…*

I have to admit, however, with some embarrass-ment, and more shame, sitting on the rough-riding bus, that the call of the bathroom has become urgent oftener now and no longer do I have the urge that I used to have to pacify my urge to pee. With a mind that no longer distinguishes amongst faces and nor does it recognize one address from the other, a mind that does not place a face against a telephone number, I watch my own sloughing off of habits of cleanliness, I watch my own deterioration, my own incapacities; the increasing difficulty to unscrew the cap of a plastic bottle; trying to unscrew the cap of the gin bottle; reaching up to take frozen food from the refrigerator; or to accept the offer of space in a lineup at the cinema; and beneath it all, there is my increasing urge to pee, to empty, to void myself. Would those who offer me such consideration want to help me pee? To help me into the void? Full of good-willed unawareness. I resent all such gestures, especially when they come from young women. Not many women my age express these pleasantries. No woman of my age has ever offered me her seat. I presume it is because we are in the same boat, a boat that more and more refuses to float.

In the Sixties, I lived in many cities in America: in New Haven, Williamstown, and in Boston; and in the South, in Durham, North Carolina; in Bloomington, Indiana, and in Austin, Texas. In those cities and towns, in America, not many people got up to offer any black person their seat. I lived through the years of the determination of that black woman, Rosa Parks, who refused to surrender her seat in the "white section" of a bus in Selma, Alabama. Not being in blackface or in anybody's face back then, I chose to sit, voluntarily, in the "black section."

Here in Toronto in those self-same Sixties, I was crossing Hoskin Avenue from Trinity College and I was wearing the college's soccer colours and I took up my position as centre forward. I did not score a goal; but I was called "off-side" three times during the match; and when the final whistle was blown, and the game was over on the Front Campus pasture, I wallowed in the cheers of the cheerleaders chosen from the beautiful first-year women students; and I headed back to Trinity College with victory in my muscles and in my loins, to the dining room at the college; and as a new resident in the college, halfway to my new home, I turned right instead of left, and after I reached Yonge Street, that was the name on the telephone pole, I guessed that I had made the wrong turn. I corrected that and turned right but it was long after the last plate of white fish and mashed potatoes in a white thin sauce had been served and eaten in the dining hall that I realized that I was lost. I began in this town by being lost, standing at the corner of Bloor and Yonge in my football uniform.

And here I am, fifty-nine years later, on this same corner on a cold November evening, peeling back the years ever further beyond Trinity College to a time still in Barbados when I was strong enough to run four races – the 100 yards, the 220 yards, the 440 yards and the 880 yards – and the long jump in one afternoon and come first in each and then to be crowned "Victor Ludorum," Champion of the Games, who now finds himself on Bloor Street, meeting himself face to Kiwi face, in the show window of a specialty men's clothing store, Harry Rosen's, and I find it natural to think of T.S. Eliot who we studied during those school days and what he said about trousers and old men:

I grow old… I grow old…
I shall wear the bottoms of my trousers rolled.
Shall I part my hair behind? Do I dare to eat a peach?

I ate two peaches this morning. A ladies' magazine had told me that peaches would lengthen my life, but they are my favourite fruit anyway. I like the sweet sensual tickle of hairs kissing my mouth, but now I have to wonder what Eliot's caution meant and still means, the way we look so eagerly, with such yearning, for our future before we have even got a decent look at our present, this present where in blackface I eat a peach and wear my trousers rolled and mount a stair hoping to see a face above the stair, hoping for fairness if not friendliness, as I did back in my college days, when I stood at the top of a stairs on a stoop in a complete silence, hearing the creaking of startled shoes; the heavy sound of a dead lock, as I managed to read a well-written notice, not much larger than a tea-time calling card, stuck with Scotch tape to an inside pane of glass in the heavy, grand mahogany double door: NO COLOUREDS.

On the door itself, written in an uneven hand, the assertion, or the wish: JESUS BLESS THIS HOME.

Having come through such disappointments, having lived through flushes of, if not constant, anger and disdain for more than fifty years, having taken my place on the back of the bus and then gracefully accepted my place at the front, I have witnessed my share of deterioration of the spirit, of the body. I have seen deterioration and disintegration not only in other men, those dark pouches of disappointment beneath the eyes that they blame on their livers, but increasing fragility, as a state in itself, a fragility in my leg, my leg like life itself, covered by an infestation of scabs. And scabs that hatch. And the bone seen peeping through the flesh. And the flesh has become paper beneath my grey trousers that are loose and baggy, three sizes too large for my body, my shrunken body. It is an act of faith, this determination to stay alive while we watch ourselves shrink, doing my best, as an act of the denial of death and dying by assertively wearing my paisley scarf that catches the sunlight of the mid-afternoon, brown, grey, maroon, gold dots, commas in the design of this scarf, a silk scarf glorious and aristocratic, which is still easy for me, for I used to be a man who was studied in the taking of time, even in my years of schooling, to arrive at an aristocratic bearing; for I always wore for public appearances charcoal-grey trousers with an almost indiscernible thin vertical stripe in them; a white shirt with the front stiffened by starch, and a very hot iron, a white shirt worn in dress attire with mother-of-pearl studs; and a black silk jacket, single-breasted, custom-made, in a conservative English cut, being a practising gentleman of letters, of which I knew there were and are none too many in our time, bedecking myself in such an outfit and variations of it to assert the relishing of this aristocratic self, which makes me now feel the full weight of my bladder upon me, feel the apprehension of wetness, the apprehension of the stench of pure pee and the loss of all such earned dignity as I have, earned in the deepest sense, as one earns day to day a living. I shift from foot to foot, trying to take the weight off my bladder, which suddenly has the weight of all my past years, while at the same time I try to tighten my legs, to tense my whole body, to tense my mind, try to think of elsewhere; I go over the alphabet, from A to ZED... from A to ZEE... refusing to surrender to my body, to fragility, refusing incontinence, refusing to give in to any sign that all is lost, trying to remember so simple a thing as balance, the perfect balance that accrues to being young, along, of course, with the unknowingness that also accrues to being young; but now, being old, being one of *de old folks*, no matter where I rest or reside I have lost nearly all sense of balance, have lost my focus, lost even the quickness of the eye required to read the number on my house from inside a moving taxi, that number that I myself screwed into my green-painted front door, emerald green so I can alert some driver who has picked me up, who cannot speak my language, to the fact that We are Here, I am Here! "Here-here!" Home! As I shout, "Green," and we keep going, passing by the door, having to stop and back up, being fortunate for me that there is only one door on this street that is painted green, such taxi drivers telling me, "You? Sure? Okay? If you know where it is you going…"

The last time the driver letting me out to stand on the sidewalk like a lord, a landlord, outside my own door as I revised the muddle of my thoughts by revisiting the number of steps up the staircase inside the house that climbs from the front door, up… up… up… up… up… up… up… up… up… up… up… up… thirteen steps… an unlucky number!… and at the first floor top step turn right; and up… and I do this each time that I return home; and I wonder if the young woman who offered me her seat climbs an exact number of steps to reach her bedroom every night?

High-stepping. I am tormented by yearned-for memories of my own high-stepping, tormented because everything remembered that gives me pleasure also becomes a torment to this black man who I admit is myself, absurd in blackface, toying with the metal wing opener to his Kiwi can, who only wants, when all is said and done, to sit for an hour in a large single bathtub, to soak, in hot suds, in contentment, in comfort and ease of heart, a heart that is beating hard, having climbed another fourteen steps, having gone round a corner in a hallway in order to get to my third-floor bedroom; and although the bones in my knees do not creak and crack, I am aware that so much time is passing quickly; each stair reminding me of time, a step, a stair, an inch gained, an inch lost; all things being equal, I like my stairs. These stairs are my country. My country for an old man. I like the dignity that comes from having had the will to set my body straight, in an erect posture, if only for a moment, in order to climb...

To where I lie on my back on my bed; and I make myself raise each leg; and count to thirty, for each leg, and I huff and puff during these calisthenics that I've come to believe in as being good for me, and then my legs plop-down on the bed, a remembrance of when I ran five races, meanwhile forgetting where my cell-phone is so's to call in case of emergency alone so high up in my house... But even so, if I had my cellular phone, all the names in my pocket diary are the names of friends dead, or nearly all of them dead. Dark casualties:

"… and Tom? Whu' happen to Tom?"

"He dead."

"… and when last you see Dick?"

"Dick gone, too."

"That is life. That is the life bequeath to all o' we."

"To all o' we!"

"I hate like arse getting old…"

"Who-else dead? One foot in the grave…?"

I dial a number, and a deep-throated hum, a misplayed bass note on an organ, takes over…

"… the number you have dialed, is no longer in service."

But I am still here, yes, still in service; and glad to be, even if I am *way down upon the ribber* in this land of the living where I one day lately, on a whim, went searching through old letters and older pocket diaries determined to seek out evidence of the living, to seek out all those still whinnying with us, their names in alphabetical order, the names of men and women with whom I grew up and also men and women in this alien country of silent people who do not open their front windows and say, "Mawnin, neighbour!" And so, as if the day I did this seeking out of names was actually the Day of Dead Souls, Ash Wednesday, I called their names, one by one. Down upon a river, up a creek they came, to let me mark the foreheads of my friends as each appeared before me in my bathroom mirror. I marked their brows with a penitential thumb smear of Kiwi black polish: Grace Sin-Hill. Dalton Guiler. Superintendent Boyce. Mewreel Sealey. Judy Thomas. Rudolph Hinds... I remember him, one of the best of tenors in Barbados. D. Parris. Everton Weekes (now Sir Everton Weekes). Richie Haynes (now Sir Richard Haynes). Jill Shephard. Bruce LaPorte, former Director of Black Studies at Yale University, Edward Cumberbatch, one of the best half-milers on the island during my time, running on a hot afternoon track, marked in staggered lanes... and Malcolm X, Roy McMurtry (Judge of the Supreme Court), Norman Mailer, Morley, wagging his cane at me, telling me, "First, you outlive the bastards, then you outwrite them,"... all such as these rising up in my mirror full of pride but marked by penitence, standing in their youth like standing in a river to surrender their seats to me, singing along with me, *dere's whu de old folks stay*, and among them, many beautiful women. Yes, beautiful. Surrendering. Yes, but on what grounds was this surrender made in my favour? Grounds that made me and still make me suspicious. Why does this unalloyed kindness bring out in me such suspicion?

It is the raw suspicion that I am a mere hindrance, to be helped as a way of avoidance, a suspicion that I do not seem to be an elderly, well-dressed West Indian gentleman... "an older man," a phrase used and regarded as a term of dignity and respect back in Barbados but here, in Toronto, there is no doff of the hat, no pleasant smile on the face, no wave of the hand. Suspicious that here in this country, in the privacy of the heart, I am regarded as "an old piece o' shit!" as my feet stumble and slip and slide on the moving steps of an escalator, or, upon my walking into a revolving door, being caught in the door by the rude disregard of the person ahead of me, so that, given the cautiousness common to old men, I freeze and become stiff, and I look as if I am dead – a corpse in a revolving door – and I go round two times more, against my will, sometimes three more carousel times!... before I dare to slip out and disappear in a silence of self-accusation and shame, completely bewildered as I hear from a distance the lazy lapping of waves at the edge of a beach where there is the smell of saltiness after a wave has died and the soft whisper of that dying breath touches my own lips with the fire of an unexpected kiss. A kiss that tells me that I love life. I love life even as I embrace several wishes of the way I would like to die, to die in my sleep, in the embrace of sleep, where I would be insensitive to what is going on around me... But in the meantime... it is this "meantime," my God, that kills me. This mean-time state of slow-moving uselessness like a sudden slap of blindness, this meantime in which so it seems I am having to relearn, like a child, all the things I have taken for granted, that I take for granted on Bloor Street on this damp November Saturday late afternoon, when I look up warily to see who is walking directly in my path and I pick a man, with my warning antennae, out of the strolling crowd. He too is slow. He too is shaking. He tries to control two walking sticks. They wobble as he walks. He's hardly walking. Shuffling and stumbling. He raises the walking stick in his left hand, to greet me. Something like crazed glee, huge relief in his eyes at seeing me. Certainly I recognize the man. But I do not understand why, of all the people to slip in and out of my memory, I should be confronted by this man. The stick in his left hand waves. I do not know if this is enthusiasm. Or threat. "Dave, short for Davenport. My name is Davenport. Windsor-hyphen-Britain." Dave! Oh God, oh God! From Trinidad. We were at U of T together. 1955. The stick in his right hand joins the other stick, waving his greeting. I pretend I do not recognize him. I am in blackface. Shining face. Shining with youngness. Doing my imitation of Al Jolson. He stops in my path. He is smiling. He is happy to see me. He is blocking me. I read his happiness at meeting his old friend. But I move around him. Out of his path. *My heart is turning ebber*. His mouth is open. I raise my right arm and say, like I used to in those civil right days, "Do you know what time it is?" His mouth hangs more open.

I have spotted a taxi. The taxi stops. "Where you going, old man?" the taxi driver calls out to me in a foreign accent, leaning across the front seat. I guess he is from Somalia. Or Nigeria. Or Niger. Or Zimbabwe. Or another country in Africa where they held the slaves before they packed them into small holds. Before they were shipped out on the passage to American and the West Indies.

Immediately, I resent this African, calling me an old man, when I am trying to cut years off my life; in protest against girls and women who offer me their seats on crowded buses, and in the subway; and in long lineups; and such meetings as this, meeting up, unsuspecting, with old lost friends, who, immediately in their flesh, in their deterioration held up by two walking sticks, remind me of how inevitably and finally lost I am. *Swanee*, I tell the driver. Take me to Swanee.

Sang Kim of Toronto is a restaurateur and writer. He is the author of *A Dream Called Laundry* and *Ballad of a Karaoke Cowboy*, and is currently working on *Woodly Allen Ate My Kimchi*, a candid and hilarious look behind-the-scenes at some of the top restau-  rants in Ontario, and is slated to launch in late 2014. He is also co-director of the Small Press of Toronto (SPoT) – a biannual book fair that takes place at a variety of venues across the city of Toronto, celebrating small press writers and publishers from all over the country – as well as the creator/host of *Cook/Book*, a photography and cookbook project that includes some of Canada's most prominent and emerging writers preparing their favourite meals.

 **George McWhirter** was born and raised in Belfast, Northern Ireland. He has lived and worked in England, Germany, Spain and Mexico. He is the author of ten books of poetry, eight books of short and long fic- tion, and four books of translation. Literary recognitions include the Commonwealth Poetry Prize (shared with Chinua Achebe), the Ethel Wilson Fiction Prize, the F.R. Scott Translation Prize. He served as the inaugural Poet Laureate of Vancouver.

David Somers is a Winnipeg writer. He cut his teeth in the writing game as a reporter for small-town newspapers in Manitoba and has spent the last thirty years working as a  carpenter, farmhand, dishwasher, and bar- tender around the world.

Leon Rooke of Toronto is the author of seven novels, sixteen short story collections, two poetry volumes, and several stage plays, among other works. Also an artist, his paintings and sculptures show at Toronto's Fran Hill Gallery. Recognitions include a Governor General's Award (*Shakespeare's Dog*), the Canada-Australia prize, the W.O. Mitchell prize, a CBC Fiction Award, the North Carolina Literature Award, and two ReLits (poetry and short fiction).

Helen Marshall of Toronto is an author, editor, and bibliophile. In 2011 she released *Skeleton Leaves*, a collection that was jury-selected for the Preliminary Ballot of the Bram Stoker Award for excellence in Horror, nominated for a Rhysling Award for Science

Fiction Poetry, and won the Aurora Award for best Canadian speculative poem. In 2012, she released her debut short story collection, *Hair Side, Flesh Side*, an exploration of history, memory, and the cost of creating art. It has been shortlisted for a 2013 Aurora Award. Her writing has been published in a range of anthologies and magazines including *Tor.com, Paper Crow, The Year's Best Canadian Speculative Fiction and Poetry* and *The Year's Best Dark Fantasy and Horror*.

Priscila Uppal is a Toronto poet, fiction writer and York University professor. Among her books are nine collections of poetry, most recently, *Ontological Necessities* (shortlisted for the $50,000 Griffin Poetry Prize), *Traumatology, Successful Tragedies: Poems 1998-2010, Winter Sport: Poems* and *Summer Sport: Poems*; the critically-acclaimed novels *The Divine Economy of Salvation* and *To Whom It May Concern*; and the study *We Are What We Mourn: The Contemporary English-Canadian Elegy*. Her work has been published internationally and translated into Croatian, Dutch, French, Greek, Italian, Korean and Latvian. She is also the editor of several anthologies, including *The Best Canadian Poetry in English 2001*, *The Exile Book of Poetry in Translation: 20 Canadian Poets Take on the World*, and *The Exile Book of Canadian Sports Stories*.

Yakos Spiliotopoulos of Toronto is second-generation Canadian, of Greek origin. His work explores aspects of modern Greece and Greek culture, as well as the immigrant experience in Canada.

Greg Hollingshead of Toronto has published six books of fiction, among them *The Roaring Girl*, *The Healer*, and *Bedlam*. He has won the Governor General's Award and the Rogers Writers' Trust Fiction Prize and been shortlisted for the Giller Prize. He is Professor Emeritus at the University of Alberta and director of the Writing Studio at the Banff Centre. Recently he has served as Chair of the Writers' Union of Canada. In 2007 he was awarded the Lieutenant Governor of Alberta Gold Medal for Excellence in the Arts. In 2012 he received the Order of Canada.

Matthew R. Loney of Toronto is a graduate of the University of Toronto's MA in English and Creative Writing (2009). Loney's work has appeared in a range of North American publications including Fernwood's anthology of political short fiction *Everything is So Political* and Clark-Nova's anthology *Writing Without Direction: 10 1/2 short stories by Canadian authors under 30.* He recently published in India and Hong Kong.

Rob Peters of Vancouver has had short stories and essays appear in *Event, SubTerrain, Joyland,* and *The Tyee.* He was nominated for the 2012 Journey Prize and placed second in the Vancouver International Writers Festival 2008 Short Story Contest. He recently completed his MFA at the University of British Columbia, where he was awarded the Earle Birney and Brissenden Scholarships in Creative Writing. His journalism has appeared in publications around Vancouver.

Liz Windhorst Harmer of Hamilton, Ontario, has had her stories appear in *Little Fiction* and *The Challenge of Three*, an anthology featuring the winners of the 2010 GritLit competition. She has an MA in English from McMaster University, and she has worked with Richard Bausch and Joan Barfoot through the Humber School for Writers. She is completing a first novel.

Austin Clarke of Toronto is a Bajan-born Canadian novelist, short story writer, and memoirist. Winner of the Giller, Commonwealth and Trillium prizes for his novel *The Polished Hoe*, Clarke has published 10 novels, six short story collections and three non-fiction works including the memoir *Growing Up Stupid Under the Union Jack.* He is also the winner of the Toronto Book Award for his novel *More* and the Rogers Communications

Writers' Development Trust Prize for Fiction for *The Origin of Waves*. In 2012 he was honoured with the $10,000 Harbourfront Festival Prize for lifetime achievement. He is a member of the Order of Canada. His first poetry collection, *Where the Sun Shines Best*, was published in 2013. He releases the short story collection, *They Never Told Me, and Other Stories*, with Exile Editions in Autumn 2013.